The Beast
and Other Tales

Northwestern University Press
www.nupress.northwestern.edu

Support for this publication came in part through the Global Humanities Initiative,
which is jointly supported by Northwestern University's Buffett Institute for Global
Studies and Kaplan Institute for the Humanities.

Printed in the United States of America

10 9 8 7 6 5 4 3 2 1

Library of Congress Cataloging-in-Publication Data

Names: Arbaud, Joseph d', 1874–1950, author. | Zonana, Joyce, translator.
Title: The beast : and other tales / Jóusè d'Arbaud ; translated from the Provençal by
    Joyce Zonana.
Other titles: Bèstio dóu Vacarés. English
Description: Evanston, Illinois : Northwestern University Press, 2020. | Includes
    bibliographical references.
Identifiers: LCCN 2020015272 | ISBN 9780810143128 (paperback) | ISBN
    9780810143135 (ebook)
Classification: LCC PQ2601.R24 B413 2020 | DDC 849.352—dc23
LC record available at https://lccn.loc.gov/2020015272

The Beast
and Other Tales

Jóusè d'Arbaud

Translated from the Provençal
by Joyce Zonana

NORTHWESTERN UNIVERSITY PRESS
EVANSTON, ILLINOIS

CONTENTS

ACKNOWLEDGMENTS

Thanks, especially, to Brigitte Curdel, who introduced me to *La Bèstio dóu Vacarés / La Bête du Vaccarès* during my initial visit to the Camargue and later gifted me with her precious first edition of d'Arbaud's novella. During my stay at the Cacharel Hotel in the very landscape where *La Bèstio* is set, owner Denys Colomb de Daunant generously shared with me his enthusiasm for d'Arbaud. Jacques Guillaume, the gracious owner of the Camargue Librairie in Les Saintes-Maries-de-la-Mer, sold me my first copies of *La Bèstio* and *La Caraco*. I first learned about Henri Bosco's indebtedness to d'Arbaud at the Fonds de Documentation Henri Bosco in Nice, and I am grateful to the librarians there—Angela Maffre and Catherine Hadjopoulou—for their tireless assistance. Michele F. Levy and Jimmy Griffin were enthusiastic and perspicacious first readers; Michael J. Piecuch offered unfailing sustenance and support. The Corporation of Yaddo granted me a glorious residency that allowed me to fully enter d'Arbaud's imagined universe, and the New York Public Library made its bountiful resources readily available. Rajeev Kinra and Laura Brueck of Northwestern University's Global Humanities Initiative selected this work for the Global Humanities Translation Prize, awarded by the Buffett Institute for Global Affairs and the Alice Kaplan Institute for the Humanities. Anne Gendler at Northwestern University Press was a scrupulous and sensitive editor, the best one could hope for. Deep thanks to all of these and to many more, including, especially, Alyson Waters and Paul Eprile.

> You need to know the Camargue and to have led a gardian's life to understand how a single thought can possess a man's soul when, with no answering voice and attended only by his dreams, he rides alone on horseback through the sansouiro, like a ship a-sail on a desert sea.
>
> —JÓUSÈ D'ARBAUD

I first encountered Jóusè d'Arbaud's *La Bèstio dóu Vacarés/La Bête du Vaccarès* in the fall of 2014 when I traveled to southern France in hopes of acquiring a better grasp of a novel I was translating, Henri Bosco's *Malicroix*, set in the Camargue. Although I understood Bosco's words, I wanted to see for myself the remote region he so vividly evoked. Only then, I thought, could I accurately render the book's language.

During that first visit, my hostess, Brigitte Curdel, a poet-photographer who had moved to the Camargue from Paris, handed me a battered first edition of *La Bèstio*. It had been given to her, she told me, by an elderly neighbor, a woman who had lived there her whole life. "If you want to know the Camargue," Brigitte said, "you need to read this." More words, I thought, when what I wanted were experiences. Still, I opened the book and was staggered by what I found. D'Arbaud's words *became* my experiences, my initiation into the Camargue—as much an inward state of mind as an outward location.

Everywhere I went during that first trip, I discovered signs of d'Arbaud: the main square in Les Saintes-Maries-de-la-Mer, the Camargue's central village, bore his name; the bookstore in that square prominently displayed his works; and more than one person boasted that they reread *La Bèstio* every year. "C'est le plus beau livre sur la solitude," one woman told me. "It's the most beautiful book about solitude." Later I would learn that both Jean Giono and Henri Bosco, among others, had been deeply influenced by d'Arbaud; indeed, Bosco's *Malicroix* and other novels of his incorporate language and scenes from the writing of the man he honored as a primary source of his inspiration. And yet, outside the Camargue, d'Arbaud is largely unknown today.

I did not realize it at the time, but Brigitte's gesture when she shared d'Arbaud's masterpiece with me echoed the opening gesture of the novella's frame, when "Tall Tony," an elderly bull herder—known as a "gardian" in the Camargue—offers to give his master the tattered handwritten journal passed down in his family for generations. Intrigued by the five-hundred-year-old notebook he inherits from Tall Tony, the master—a "manadier" or rancher—turns editor, deciphering the manuscript's "astonishing mix of Provençal, French, and poor Church Latin" to present it "as faithfully as possible" to his twentieth-century readers.

Like that nameless manadier-editor, I too was drawn to this purportedly ancient yet strikingly contemporary text, rooted in the Camargue of the Middle Ages yet reaching forward to our imperiled twenty-first-century planet. Also like him, I have worked to prepare a text faithful to the original yet accessible to an English-speaking audience—because, as the novella's frame editor urges, the book's "peculiar mystery" and "evident sincerity" have much to recommend them, containing as they do a message that is vital to our time. This is a book to be shared, to be passed from hand to hand, to be lived with, read, reread, dreamt. How fitting, then, that it has been chosen for Northwestern University Press's Global Humanities Translation Prize. Perhaps *La Bèstio dóu Vacarés* will now claim its rightful place among the humanities texts we turn to for sustenance; perhaps Jóusè d'Arbaud will be recognized as "among the masters of world literature," as Alphonse V. Roche—a scholar of modern Provençal who taught at Northwestern— called him some eighty years ago.

In 1926, Jóusè d'Arbaud, commonly referred to as "Joseph d'Arbaud," published *The Beast of Vacarés* in a bilingual Provençal and French edition. At that time, the Camargue delta where he set his mythic tale was a desolate region of southern France, a flat, marshy tract between the two branches of the Rhône (known as *lou grand* and *lou pichot Rose* in Provençal), reaching south from the Roman walls of Arles to the windswept beaches of the Mediterranean. Peopled by a handful of solitary herders, hunters, and fishermen, it was home to droves of wild black bulls, white horses, and pink flamingos.

Today, nearly a hundred years later, the Camargue is much the same: a wide-open terrain of blue lagoons, green marshes, and white sands where bulls, horses, and birds freely roam. The once tiny seaside village of Les Saintes-Maries-de-la-Mer—immortalized in paintings by Van Gogh and known for its annual Gypsy pilgrimage bringing together diverse Romani peoples from across Europe—has grown to accommodate a burgeoning tourist trade. Commercial rice paddies occupy parts of the once open prairie, but conservationists have succeeded in keeping much of the barren landscape intact. Even the village of "Les Saintes"—named for the three Marys (Mary Magdalene, Mary Jacobe, and Mary Salome) said to have arrived from the Holy Land in a rudderless, sail-less boat, bringing Christianity to Provence—retains its low buildings with their red tile roofs and whitewashed walls. Here the eye ranges over a flat, glimmering expanse, where fresh winds fill the lungs as low clouds scud across the encircling sky.

The Camargue remains a place for mirages and dreams, a liminal end-of-the-world kind of place where land, sea, and sky merge; where all boundaries—between fiction and fact, poetry and prose, human and animal, sacred and profane, inside and out, even masculine and feminine—dissolve: the perfect, indeed, only possible, setting for d'Arbaud's tale of an improbable yet necessary meeting between man and myth. "Could I have found it elsewhere?" d'Arbaud wrote many years later of the Beast he claimed to have met south of the Vaccarès, the vast lagoon that spreads northward from Les Saintes: "I felt [the Beast's] presence beneath the thickets of juniper and mastic; beneath the thorny, interlaced vines; in the troubling, serene solitude; facing the bare horizons where waves of mirage trembled and shone."

Early in *La Bèstio*, d'Arbaud uses a note to suggest the force that animates his work. The narrator, a fifteenth-century gardian named Jaume Roubaud, who struggles to recount his inexplicable and—as he keeps reminding us—inexpressible experiences, mentions *la Vièio ié danso* ("The Old Dancer"), the local term for the frequent mirages found in the Camargue. D'Arbaud explains:

> These mirages . . . begin with a vibration in the air, a trembling that runs along the ground and seems to make the images dance; it spreads into the distance in great waves that reflect the dark thickets. How not to see in this mysterious Vièio, dancing in the desert sun, a folk memory of the untouchable wild goddess, ancient power, spirit of solitude, once considered divine, that remains the soul of this great wild land?

It is this "untouchable wild goddess," the "spirit of solitude" and mystery, who haunts *The Beast of Vacarés*. She is not quite the strange Beast the narrator encounters on the *sansouiro*, the Camargue's distinctive salt flats dotted with tufts of samphire, a low-growing salt-tolerant succulent also known as saltwort or glasswort. Yet her dazzling presence shapes the credulous gardian's every syllable. Is what he sees an illusion, a dangerous and deceptive mirage born from his isolation—a devil perhaps? Or is it a vision of truth, a demigod, as the Beast itself claims? Whatever one concludes, the Beast, like *La Vièio*, is unmistakably an "ancient power" that transfixes all who glimpse it. Together, *La Vièio* and the Beast invite us to remember a time when divinity danced upon the earth.

Born in 1874 in the Provençal village of Meyrargues to a poet mother and a landowner father, Jóusè d'Arbaud was educated at the Collège des Jésuites Saint-Joseph in Avignon. He studied law in Aix-en-Provence, but soon lost interest in a legal career as he began publishing poems and editing a literary journal. In 1897, at the age of twenty-three, the young man shocked family and friends when he left the cosmopolitan world of Aix for the lonely Camargue, where he set himself up as a manadier, tending a herd of wild bulls and writing poems in Provençal.

In moving to the Camargue, d'Arbaud was following in the footsteps of his cousin, the Marquis Folco de Baroncelli-Javon (1869–1943), an activist writer and manadier who codified the traditions of the Camargue and glorified the life of the gardian, simultaneously cowboy and Indian. Baroncelli had formed friendships with Native Americans in Buffalo Bill's traveling Wild West show and was convinced that the inhabitants of the Camargue, including the Roma—whom he championed—were kin to the Indians of North America. It was Baroncelli who created the *Nacioun Gardiano*, the ceremonial fraternity of nattily dressed gardians who gallantly perform on their white horses at public gatherings; it was he too who persuaded local Church officials to permit the Roma to honor their patron saint, Sara, during their springtime pilgrimage to Les Saintes. Celebrated in an annual *Journée Baroncelli*, his influence continues to be felt throughout the region.

In choosing to write in Provençal, d'Arbaud was furthering the project of his literary mentor, the man he called *Maître*, "Master"—Frédéric Mistral (1830–1914), the Nobel Prize–winning author of *Miréio* (*Mireille*) and *Lou Poème dóu Rose* (*The Poem of the Rhône*) and founder, in 1854, of the Felibrige, a coterie of writers dedicated to reviving Provençal, or Occitan. Although Provençal, the language of the Troubadors, was the first literary vernacular in Europe, it had declined toward the end of the Middle Ages and by the nineteenth century had all but disappeared in its written form. The regionalist poets and fiction writers of the Felibrige—including d'Arbaud's mother, Azalaïs d'Arbaud, the first female *felibresso*—sought to re-create the glory of old "Occitania," resisting the centralizing, nationalist agenda of the French government based in Paris.

The young d'Arbaud's allegiance to the Camargue and to Provençal was political, aesthetic, and ultimately, profoundly and passionately spiritual—an allegiance to Christian and pagan ancestors who once walked that land.

This is made most clear in his manifesto of an early poem, "Esperit de la Terro" ("Spirit of the Earth"), from which it is worth quoting at length:

> *S'ère vengu dóu tèms que li raço pacano*
> *Batien touto la terro en butant si troupèu . . .*

"If I had come in the time of pagan peoples / Who roamed the whole earth as they drove their herds";

> *Se lis estello o la sentido dóu bestiau*
> *M'aguèsson, un bèu jour, adu dins lis engano . . .*

"If the stars or the scent of the beasts / had one day led me to the samphire,"

> *Aqui, auriéu planta mon tibenèu de lano*
> *E tra sus lou sablas la pèiro dóu fougau.*

"I would have placed my woolen tent right here / And set my hearthstone on this sand."

> *S'ère vengu dóu tèms que, pèr èstre quaucun,*
> *N'i avié proun d'èstre un ome e d'ama soun terraire,*
> *Me sariéu fa basti, liuen de tout, pèr li Fraire,*
> *Un grand castèu de pèiro en raro di palun.*

"If I had come at the time when, to be someone / All you had to do was to be a man and to love your land / I would have built, far from everything, near the Monks / A great stone chateau beside the marsh."

> *Toubaire e cavalié, mai libre Prouvençau,*
> *Afeciouna pèr lou bèn-dire e la bouvino,*
> *Toustèms auriéu mescal dins moun amo latino*
> *Li pouèmo di pastre e di libre gregau.*

"Poet and horseman, but free Provençal / In love with bulls and beautiful words / I would have always mingled, in my Latin soul / The herders' poems with the Greeks'."

> *Mai siéu vengu d'un tèms que se respèton gaire*
> *La liberta di pastre e li trobo di vièi . . .*

"But I have come at a time when no one respects / The freedom of the herder and the songs of the ancients . . ."

Amo de nòsti vièi enclauso dins sis os,
Esperit de la terro ounte dormon li raço,
Pèr nous autre, t'a mai bandi foro dóu cros
La forço dóu soulèu e la voues de l'aurasso.

"Soul of our ancestors enclosed in their bones / Spirit of the earth where the people sleep / For us you have still made arise from the tomb / The strength of the sun and the voice of the wind."

Vaqui perqué dins lou reiaume de la sau,
Vira de-vers la mar espère ta vengudo,
Per te mies apara, per te presta d'ajudo,
Me siéu fa gardo-bèstio e cante prouvençau.

"Which is why, in the kingdom of salt, / Turned toward the sea, I await your arrival, / In order to better defend you, to give you my aid, / I have made myself a gardian and I sing in Provençal."

"I have made myself a gardian and I sing in Provençal." It may at first be difficult to understand why these two activities—bull herding and Provençal poetizing—should be so linked, and so important to d'Arbaud and his mentors. Yet for writers of the Felibrige, they were both thought to embody the oppressed soul or spirit of Provence: bull herding, because bulls' presence in the Mediterranean goes back thousands of years to a time when they were worshipped as gods; Provençal, because the language—not a dialect or patois of French as it has been called by some—was the ancestral tongue of the *pays d'oc*, still spoken by the common people. Both the culture of bulls—*bouvino*—and the *langue d'oc* were threatened with extinction. In Provence, many of the activities associated with the raising of bulls had been turned into games for popular entertainment. Among these, the traditional *course Camarguaise*, for which there is evidence as early as the fifteenth century, did not involve killing bulls; instead, unarmed young men competed to remove a cockade from between the bulls' horns, shaped, unlike Spanish bulls' horns, in the form of a lyre. Spanish bullfighting (*corrida de muerte*) was a recent import, along with the Spanish bulls themselves. But in the late nineteenth and early twentieth centuries, all bull games in France were under attack by the Church, the central government, and the S.P.D.A., the society for the prevention of cruelty to animals. At the same time, the use of Provençal was forbidden in public schools. Writing in *Le Feu* in the 1920s, d'Arbaud urges his fellow Provençal citizens to resist anti-bullfighting propaganda and regulations that threaten "the dignity, the freedom, and the very soul of our land"; in almost the same breath, he celebrates the "miracle of this defeated, persecuted language, systematically debased, which lives, which lasts." "The Midi will keep its *courses de taureaux*," he promises, "just as it will keep its language and character."

The region we today call Provence—the *pays d'oc*—did not officially become a part of France until 1486. In 1539 an ordinance decreed that official documents must be written in French, beginning the suppression of the native tongue. But members of the Felibrige believed that the domination of the South by the North had begun several centuries earlier, during the Albigensian Crusades of the thirteenth century. A series of especially brutal wars, these crusades were initiated by Pope Innocent III to eliminate Catharism, an anticlerical movement that flourished primarily in Provence. Most of the crusaders came from the North; in 1226, the troops were led by King Louis VIII. The Inquisition was an outgrowth of these crusades; whole towns were massacred and scores of people burned alive for supposed heresies. (When the fifteenth-century narrator of *The Beast* notes that he lives "in an age when Church courts are rarely lenient, when anything wondrous soon reeks of flames," we sense his intimate knowledge of these horrors.) The Albigensian Crusades have been called the first "ideological genocide"; to the Felibres, they were not so much a religious war as a war of expansion and extermination. But as Mistral writes, "what really was subdued . . . was less the South materially speaking, than the spirit of the South."

Nowhere was the "spirit of the South" more alive than in the Camargue, where the ancestral occupation of bull herder still flourished and where the influence of the central government was least felt. Baroncelli believed that "the gardians and people of Saintes-Maries-de-la-Mer were the last guardians of our language." D'Arbaud's decision to herd and to sing in this lonely marshland had a compelling logic; it was the best place and the best way to promote the return of the "soul of our ancestors," the "spirit of the earth."

Yet d'Arbaud's choice meant that he would have a long wait before receiving national or international recognition. Among the Felibres, he was regarded as Mistral's successor, the South's "purest" writer; Mistral himself declared, "you are above them all." In 1906, d'Arbaud was elected laureate of the Felibrige for his poetry collection *Li Cant palustre* (*Songs of the Marshes*), although the poems were not published as a volume until after his death in 1950. In 1913 he published *Lou Lausié d'Arle* (*The Laurels of Arles*), a collection of poems with a preface by Mistral. In 1917 d'Arbaud became editor in chief of *Le Feu, Organe du Régionalisme méditerranéen,* an important literary and political journal—*The Fire: Organ of Mediterranean Regionalism*—with which he remained actively involved as writer, editor, and director until 1937. In 1939 he was awarded the Prix Lasserre after the publication of his first book in French, *La Provence, Types et Coutumes* (*Customs and Folk of Provence*). And in 1943, he was at last honored by the Academie Française for all his writings in Provençal. His death in March 1950, marked by a stately funeral in Aix-en-Provence, brought an outpouring of praise from numerous writers and critics, including Henri Bosco.

Yet only a handful of Anglophone critics have remarked on d'Arbaud's work. In 1926, Vernon Loggins hailed *La Bèstio* as the "outstanding book of the year" in Provençal, celebrating the "rich music of the style" and calling it a "poet's book." Throughout his long career, Alphonse V. Roche championed his friend d'Arbaud, even going so far as to craft a translation of *La Bèstio* that never found a publisher. In 1947, Amy and Philip Mairet published a charming translation in the now out-of-print collection *Angels and Beasts: New Short Stories from France* edited by Denis Saurat. More recently, R. T. Sussex lauded d'Arbaud as the "Poet of the Camargue," and Patricia Merivale and Robert Zaretsky have given glancing attention to *La Bèstio.*

In her comprehensive study of d'Arbaud's masterpiece, Mireille Fouque calls it a *"roman de terroir"* and a *"conte fantastique"*—a novel of place (what we might call "regionalist" or "local color" fiction) and a tale of fantasy. On the one hand, it is crammed with realistic, prosaic details of a gardian's daily life and the flora and fauna of the Camargue, supplemented by elaborate, substantiating footnotes. On the other hand, it introduces a poetically eloquent "Beast," a fantastic creature with miraculous powers and evident literary and mythological ancestors—although, as Jean-Louis Vaudoyer points out, the classically trained d'Arbaud drew his fantasy directly from nature, unlike, say, how Maurice de Guérin constructed his *Centaure.* We fully believe in d'Arbaud's Beast as he emerges from the thickets and salt plains of the Camargue.

Much more than a *roman de terroir* or a *conte fantastique,* though, *La Bèstio* is above all an astute psychological study of a mind struggling to come to terms with an experience that challenges all its preconceived notions. The Beast the gardian meets on the sansouiro escapes categorization. Roubaud scrupulously portrays his own mental and spiritual breakdown, as he vacilates wildly between attraction and repulsion, trust and suspicion, pity and fear. The Beast is the ultimate "Other," challenging the narrator's Self. In the end, Roubaud discovers that Other within himself. Who he thought he was dissolves; a new Self emerges, burdened with the tragic realization that his transformation has come too late.

From the start, Roubaud tells us that he is writing for the future, "in the hope that one day someone more learned than I will know how to shed light on these harrowing events." He is at pains to tell the truth, to record seemingly dull day-to-day details, to ensure that no one suspect him of delirium or drunkenness. "I do not write," he repeats, "for the idle amusement of whoever might one day read me, but rather to transmit these bewildering experiences to others more equipped than I to understand and clarify them." In the end, he affirms that he is

> comforted to think that the wondrous events that troubled a poor gardian in his solitude will not be swallowed in the abyss of time, lost like so many others, and that one day someone wiser and more learned than I will come and, observing them from afar without terror, will know how to explain and understand what my ignorance alone perhaps veils from me today.

We who read these words are indeed "wiser and more learned" than the poor gardian. Less constrained by dogma, we have multiple ways of understanding the events that bewilder him; we can more easily take the Beast at its word, seeing in it an emblem of an endangered worldview that recognizes the divinity of nature and our kinship with all beings. Understanding Roubaud, we can, perhaps, avoid the tragic fate that befalls both him and his Beast. In *La Bèstio*, d'Arbaud has bequeathed us a heartbreaking tale that might save us.

The gardian's final feeling is one of remorse. This remorse also permeates the three spare short stories presented here with *La Bèstio*: "The Caraco," "Pèire Guilhem's Remorse," and "The Longline." Written and initially published in literary journals several years before *La Bèstio*, they also appeared in a bilingual edition in 1926, *La Caraco—Raconte Camarguen* (*The Caraco: Tales of the Camargue*), published by Editioun de la Revisto *Le Feu*. Set in the twentieth century, each understated tale features a solitary gardian, struggling like Roubaud to come to terms with an experience that challenges his prior worldview: the arrival of a lost Roma girl on the sansouiro; the plight of a beloved horse in the arena at Arles; the sudden appearance of a stranger at a favorite fishing hole. In "The Caraco" and "Pèire Guilhem's Remorse," the pressure of outside voices—like the voice of the Church in *La Bèstio*—keeps the gardian from following his better instincts; in "The Longline," too, the gardian succumbs to his fear of judgment by others. And in all three stories, the abyss of time and space awaits the gardians, a reflection of the abyss that plays so large a role in *La Bèstio*.

* * *

D'Arbaud, although he wrote much prose, was primarily a poet, and in my translation, I have striven to preserve the poetry of *La Bèstio*. When I first read the novella, and when I first began to translate, I worked from d'Arbaud's French text, *La Bête du Vaccarès*. But whenever I looked over to the facing Provençal page—the original—I could see that the words were not exactly the same. For example, when Roubaud's horse Clar-de-Luno swerves one evening, *sans raison* in French, "for no reason," the Provençal has *sènso rimo ni resoun*, literally "without rhyme or reason." Later, after his first full encounter with the Beast, the French has Roubaud *livré à une véritable obsession dont les alternatives et les contradictions m'épuisaient*—"given over to a true obsession, whose alternatives and contradictions exhaust" him. But in Provençal, Roubaud is *secuta pèr un veritable desvàri, que si vai-et-ven e soun bataiage me desmesoulavon*—"possessed by a true madness whose back-and-forth battering wears [him] to the bone." In this case, as in so many others, the Provençal proved more concrete, more vivid, and more alive than the French.

In at least one passage, the difference between d'Arbaud's Provençal and his French was deeply consequential, revealing the greater nuance available to him in Provençal. After an especially unsettling encounter with the Beast, the narrator Roubaud claims in French to have seen "l'être au jambes de bouc"—the goat-legged being—conducting "un sabbat de bêtes"—a sabbath of the beasts. The Provençal has him seeing "l'autre, cambu comme un bou"—the other, with the legs of a goat. "L'autre" in Provençal has the same meaning as in French—the "other." But there is an additional, regional meaning—"le diable," Mistral's dictionary tells us, the devil. Interestingly enough, this devil, "l'autre" not "l'être," conducts his sabbath from atop an "auturo," a small rise in the otherwise flat sansouiro. My solution strives to retain some of the ambiguity available in the Provençal, though the richness of d'Arbaud's language play is lost.

It may be that d'Arbaud, like Mistral, believed that French,

> born under a rainy climate, stiff, starched by the etiquette of court, shaped above all by its use among the upper classes . . . is naturally, and always will be, unlike the free disposition, bubbling character, rustic customs, lively and vivid speech of Provençal. For it is more contrived, more conventional than any other, more suitable for science, philosophy, politics, and the needs of a refined civilization.

Could d'Arbaud have *deliberately* made his French translation less powerful than his Provençal original, precisely to prove to his readers that the

Provençal language, as Mistral claimed, was "closer to Latin, more sono-rous, and more expressive than their own"? Certainly he convinced me, and so I found myself relying on Mistral's encyclopedic Provençal-French dictio-nary, *Lou Tresor dóu Felibrige*, for detailed (and often delightful) definitions of Provençal words. Whenever faced with a choice, I favored the Provençal, which, interestingly enough, had more similarities with colloquial English than with literary French. In addition, I retained the Provençal spellings for most personal and place names, hoping in this way to lure readers into d'Arbaud's landscape. In the Mistralian norm, "normo mistralenco," nouns do not inflect for number, and in most cases I have followed this conven-tion when using specific Provençal terms that can be plural or singular: clavo, radèu, manado, gaso, and Caraco. The notes at the end of the text are d'Arbaud's, explaining some Provençal terms and local customs and beliefs.

During his encounters with Roubaud, the Beast tells him that he has come to the Camargue in search of the "wild wind" he "cannot live without," the "free air and wild sky," essential to his survival. The Camargue, the Beast says, is the last place on earth that offers him what he needs. Like the Beast, like d'Arbaud, I too have been drawn back again and again—as a reader and a pilgrim, in imagination and fact—to that solitary, windswept netherland, a sort of nowhere that becomes everywhere, finding in it an openness that does indeed foster visions, allowing the "soul of our ancestors" and the "spirit of the earth" (*lou esperit de la terro*) to speak. It is my hope that this edition of *The Beast, and Other Tales* will lead readers on similar journeys, fostering similar visions.

Selected Bibliography

Arbaud, Joseph, d'. *La Bèstio dóu Vacarés / La Bête du Vaccarès*. Paris: Bernard Grasset, 1926.

———. *La Caraco / La Caraque: Raconte Camarguen*. Le Feu, 1926.

———. *La Sóuvagino / La Sauvagine*. Paris: Bernard Grasset, 1929.

———. *Li Cant Palustre / Les Chants Palustres*. Paris: Horizons de France, 1951.

Bosco, Henri. "La Camargue et sa poésie: Le pays—le peuple: Joseph d'Arbaud." *La Tunisie Française Littéraire*. November 15, 22, and 29, 1941.

Chamson, André. *Réception imaginaire de Joseph d'Arbaud: poète et gentil-homme de Camargue: Institut de France, Académie française, séance publique annuelle tenue le 19 décembre 1974*. Paris: Institut de France, 1974.

Dalgarno, Philip. "Inventing the *Petite Patrie*: The Félibrige as Nationalist Project." Senior Honors Thesis, European and Mediterranean Studies, New York University, May 2015.

Desiles, Emmanuel. "Mystique/Poète: Sur un meta-poème de Joseph d'Arbaud." *Revue d'études d'oc, La France latine* (2011): 21–31.

Durand, Bruno. *Joseph d'Arbaud: Conference prononcée à Cavaillon 19 decembre 1970*. Mistral, 1972.

Fouque, Mireille. *Étude de "la Bête du Vaccarès" de Joseph d'Arbaud*. Publications de la Faculté des lettres et des science humaines de Nice, no. 19. Nice, 1980.

Gardy, Phillippe. "Écrire la Bête ou le centaure impossible." *Revue des langues romanes* 99, no. 1 (1995): 1–18.

———. *L'exil des origins: renaissance littéraire et renaissance linguistique en pays de langage d'oc au xixième et xxième siècles*. Bordeaux: Presses Universitaire de Bordeaux, 2006.

Jouveau, Marie-Thérèse. *Joseph d'Arbaud*. Nimes: Bené, 1984.

Lafont, R. "De-qu'es aquela bèstia?" *Revue des langues romanes* 99, no. 1 (1995): 65–72.

Loggins, Vernon. "*La Bèstio dóu Vacarés* by Joseph d'Arbaud." *The Sewanee Review* 34, no. 3 (1926): 350–53.

Magrini, C., and Charles Mauron, "Satyre, faune, centaure: le personage de la Bête et ses références littéraires contemporains." *Revue des langues romanes* 99, no. 1 (1995): 19–48.

Mauron, Charles. "De Joseph d'Arbaud à Henri Bosco." *Marseille: Revue Municipale Trimestrielle*, nos. 128–29 (Premier Semestre 1982): 15–19; reprinted from no. 103 (October–December 1979).

Mauron, Marie. *Quand la Provence nous est contée par ses plus grands poètes et chroniqueurs: des troubadours à Joseph d'Arbaud*. Paris: Perrin, 1975.

Merivale, Patricia. *Pan the Goat-God: His Myth in Modern Times*. Cambridge: Harvard University Press, 1969.

Pic, F. "Bibliographie sommaire de Joseph d'Arbaud." *Revue des langues romanes* 99, no. 1 (1995): 91–107.

Roche, Alphonse V. "La Camargue et ses poètes." *The French Review* 32, no. 1 (October 1958): 32–37.

———. "Modern Provençal Literature and Joseph d'Arbaud." *Books Abroad* 16, no. 2 (Spring 1942): 131–34.

———. *Provençal Regionalism: A Study of the Movement in the "Revue Félibréenne," "Le Feu," and Other Reviews of Southern France*. Evanston, Ill.: Northwestern University Press, 1954.

Romestaing, Alain. "*La Bête du Vaccarès* de Joseph d'Arbaud: l'impossible face à face." *L'Esprit Créateur* 51, no. 4 (Winter 2011): 45–57.

Séguy, Jean-B. "De l'aliénation au fantastique: problèmes de la prose littéraire d'Oc." *Esprit* 12, no. 376 (1968): 669–83.

Sussex, R. T. "Joseph d'Arbaud, Poet of the Camargue." *Journal of the Australasian Universities Language and Literature Association* 42, no. 1 (1974): 175–84.

Zaretsky, Robert. *Cock and Bull Stories: Folco de Baroncelli and the Invention of the Camargue*. Lincoln: University of Nebraska Press, 2004.

The Beast
and Other Tales

The Beast of Vacarés

Notice

In the countryside near Nimes, on the Arles plain between the Alpilles and the Cévennes, all of us bound by our ancestral passion for bulls know that around 1904 Pèire Antòni Recoulin, nicknamed *Long-Toni*, Tall Tony, was my *baile-gardian*, head of my *manado* on the Caban lands beside *lou Grand-Rose*, the Great Rhône.

Tall Tony had a strong, supple body, topped by a sunburnt face. His head was shaved all around like a Roman's; thick gray hair crowned his temples and proconsular nape; and two small, shrewd eyes glittered fiercely under drawn eyebrows.

A good Camargo horseman and nothing more, but one whose looks made the few folks from Arles I hosted every now and then—as rarely as possible—rave about big chiefs and legionnaires.

Intelligent yet illiterate like most gardians of his day (for, at the time I am speaking of, Tall Tony was already quite old), he both respected and feared books, with a naive faith he voiced in more or less the same way each time.

I can see him now. Ordinarily muter than the carp in the *roubino*, he would suddenly take his pipe out of his mouth, roll his eyes toward the little library on the shelves of an old *estanié* in my cabin, put his pipe back in his mouth, and, after resolutely gulping down his saliva, turn toward me. I knew then, without fail, what I was about to hear.

"Books, after all! And to think that you yourself can take everything laid out on paper and bring it into your head! Now that's something I don't really understand. Learning's wonderful, I'm not saying it isn't, but it's not natural. To mount a wild horse, to tame it, to teach it the regular moves with bulls—do you need to know how to read? Read? I'm not saying it's not a beautiful thing, but sooner or later it must make your head explode."

One winter evening, after we had returned from the blind and were sipping some cool absinthe in front of a blaze of *tamarisso* while we waited for the eel *catigot* to finish simmering in its little pot over the fire, Tall Tony suddenly spoke.

3

"As soon as I'm done eating, I'll hit the hay. Duck hunting isn't worth the trouble it takes. Boots or no boots, it was no use, I got soaked dragging in one of those damn sons of bitches from the lagoon. But as for you, for sure you're going to read. Reading's a passion, like *bouvino*. I have a book of my own in Arles that might give you a thing or two to think about. I should bring it to you some day. From one end to the other, it's all written by hand, and who can say how far back it goes? It comes to me from my mother's great-uncle Galastre, a well-known gardian back then. As my wife is my witness, I've never wanted to sell this book to a soul. Here's a thought: it will be yours! Good night all. If you find yourself in it, it's because you're a good man."

As everyone knows, Tall Tony died in 1912. His widow kept his promise. It is thanks to her and to my baile's heirs that I have been able to transcribe these pages here. I wish to thank them publicly. The original manuscript is a thick notebook bound in leather and parchment, eaten away on the outside by moths and rats. The writing is yellowed, uneven, all tangled and hard to read. Some pages, once wet or exposed over time to damp and rotted by mildew, crumbled to dust like cinders when I handled them.

I have done my best to establish the text as faithfully as possible. Quite often I have had to adapt, almost to rewrite it, to make clear its astonishing mix of French, Provençal, and poor Church Latin.

The author, who by his own account lived in the middle of the fifteenth century, must have been the son of a gardian, a gardian as well, though a bit more educated than his peers. A sort of half-cleric, but in the end a poor writer, simpleminded and long-winded, as will be only too plain to readers of this narrative.

I have, as best I could, preserved the primitive tone and style, without seeking to do more than to bring together, wherever possible, the fragments of a very disjointed text. The tattered manuscript made this a laborious task.

Let it be known: literature plays no part here.

I simply sought to bring to light a tangled tale, full of obscure references and repetitions, but whose evident sincerity and peculiar mystery do not fail to add some interest.

It would most likely have been lost forever were it not for the legacy that, thankfully, Tall Tony wanted to leave me.

To some readers, I owe apologies. Perhaps they would have liked to have found here something other than this tiresome, dull transcription. Who doesn't feel the charm these days of curiosities? Who doesn't recognize the pleasure so many good minds find in senseless, convoluted fantasies?

As for me, I confess I focused all my effort on staying true to my text, while also strictly avoiding any show of learning, any concern about archaism or reconstruction, as much in setting and action as in syntax and diction.

People of good taste will, I trust, be grateful that I have not been tempted by such empty adornments.

First Chapter

In the Name of the Father, the Son, and the Holy Ghost; in the Name of Nosto-Damo-de-la-Mar and of our Santo Maries. Today, the eleventh of April in the year 1417, Holy Easter Sunday—I, Jaume Roubaud, known as *lou Grela*, the Pockmarked, baile-gardian of the manado of wild bulls that roam the Malagroi lands, the Emperiau, and lou Riege, began to write in this notebook.

As I did so, I wanted first to trace at the top of this page the Holy Sign of the Cross, symbol of my Redemption, meaning through this to solemnly swear—by my place in paradise and my eternal salvation—to the full and whole truth of everything I set down now and everything I might later be led to record.

What I have seen and heard up to today has caused me turmoil and ongoing, fevered meditation. Only too aware that I cannot myself find a natural explanation, I want to stamp my writing with a seal that sets it beyond the shadow of a doubt, in the hope that one day someone more learned than I will know how to shed light on these harrowing events.

The one or ones before whose eyes Providence unveils the secret of this book should not be surprised to find me more educated than most other gardians of wild bulls, whether masters or journeymen.

If I am not entirely illiterate, it is because from childhood I was called to the honor of the priesthood; but a tragedy forced me to abandon my studies and my hope of one day entering the dignity of the Holy Church. Still, I thank Heaven for having granted me, a little more than others, the knowledge without which I would not be able to carry out the task I have begun today.

My father, Andriéu Roubaud, gardian of *roussatino*, the Camargue horses he led through la Séuvo for the monks of Saumòdi, had an older brother, Ounourat Roubaud, who, educated under the patronage of the Father Abbot and later ordained priest, had been appointed canon in the Venerable Chapter of Nosto-Damo-de-la-Majour in Arles.

This canon Roubaud, my uncle, had a deep, fatherly affection for me. I can affirm that when I was quite young he called me to his side, where he kept me and personally instructed me in the Scriptures and ancient books, both Latin and Greek. Early mornings in church, I offered the responses for Holy Mass; I kept him company on his walks and had my place at his table as if I were truly his son. And indeed I was, by soul and affection. I had a snug bed in his white house by the arena, and I freely roamed the paths of the garden that bore such fine fruit in autumn.

Alas! Just as I was about to reach my fifteenth year, the poisonous fever ravaging the countryside carried off my benefactor. The disease attacked me as well, leaving me frail and partly disfigured.

Without my patron, I was forced to return to the manado, taking up the saddle and the *ficheiroun* again. I am not complaining. Every calling has its good and its bad. I like this one, which has been passed down from father to son in our family and which grants me a free, peaceful life.

That was also the opinion, I clearly recall, of my uncle the canon.

"See here, little one," he would say, when we had lingered at dusk on some Camargue *draio*, watching a manado fade into the distance as it was driven through the marsh by its gardians—"see here, little one, you must never, no matter to what height Providence raises you, scorn the work of your dear father. A gardian's vocation is a fine one, very much like that of the Patriarchs. After all, is it not in the vastness that a pure soul best experiences the order of the universe and the presence of God?"

Poor beloved uncle! If only he were here. I would not then be forced today to darken these pages in order to somewhat deliver myself from all that torments me. Because, to tell the truth, I do not dare confide in anyone. No, not anyone. How often, during my hours of sleeplessness or while riding alone through the mud of Malagroi, have I not resolved to confess all, to reveal everything at last? May the saints have pity and pardon me. I know very well I could not. One day, I made up my mind. I got in the saddle. But I did not have the strength to go as far as Nosto-Damo-de-la-Mar. I felt I would not know how to explain myself, neither to the Father Abbot who is so prudent nor to our priest who is so venerable. No, not even within the privacy of confession. A restraint stronger than anything seals my lips. If I were to freely recount all that haunts me, I would be taken, I believe, for a madman. We live, I must confess, in an age when Church courts are rarely lenient, when anything wondrous soon reeks of flames. I am quite certain there is neither sorcery nor Satanism in this affair. But my fear is almost as great as if there were.

It is to deliver myself, I repeat, that I write these pages today. I will know how to make sure they remain hidden until they can no longer harm me—so that, while I live, they do not betray me.

Before recounting the essence of what befell me, I must note here a disturbance that would not be worth mentioning had it not been the first sign of the growing entanglements that today leave me helpless and lost.

I was returning one evening to my cabin in the Riege, the very cabin where, hunched over this notebook, I now write.

The people of the Camargue all know the Riege. But it could be that the unknown person who one day reads me will not, or else—something I find hard to believe—the region between now and then will have been ravaged by the hand of man or the work of nature; and so, as a precaution, I feel I should devote a few brief words to the subject.

The Riege, which extends to the east and a little to the north of the celebrated church of Nosto-Damo, between the Vacarés lagoon and the coast, is a fairly narrow wooded strip, two or three leagues long, made up of little islands that emerge from the lagoons fed from the north by fresh water and opening directly onto the sea. These islands, which we call *radèu*, are covered winter and summer with a thicket of *restencle*, *óulivastre*, and those aromatic shrubs called *mourven*, among which thorny *tiragasso* vines are sometimes intertwined. Rabbit and fox abound in these woods; wildcats—*cat-fèr*—are not rare; I have even cut down wolves and some fierce lynx. Around the islands, in the lagoons where in summer *la Vièio ié danso* can be glimpsed on the dazzling salt flats that remain when the water dries, winter draws a host of wild birds: geese, ducks, teal (spawned, they say, from sea foam); not counting all the *primaio*—lapwings, plover, stilts, waders, and curlews—or flamingos, whose pink flights shimmer in summer above the vast Vacarés waters.

During the months of stifling heat, the Riege, lacking fresh water and ravaged by drought, is infested with small parasites and bloodthirsty flies that plague the bulls and horses, but because the soil is sandy, the greenery stays fresh during the winter months; when bad weather comes, the juniper thickets offer good shelter to the manado's livestock.

Mounted on my horse Clar-de-Luno, I was returning that evening from the Emperiau *baisso*, where I had gone to set duck snares. It was not yet six o'clock, but because we were in the shortest days of the year, night had already fallen. The moon was new, and so it was pitch-black out.

I should note that, to reach the radèu, it is best to use the safe crossings we call *gaso*; otherwise you risk being bogged down and perishing miserably in the thick mud that is just about everywhere in these lagoons. Gardians know this.

I had just easily forded the gaso known as Damisello. Clar-de-Luno, dry-footed on the radèu and heading straight for the cabin, was twitching his ears, slowing down, and neighing, which is how our Camargue horses let us know they recognize their surroundings and are happy to be nearing home. Suddenly, I was half lifted from the saddle by the horse's abrupt swerve. When I regained control, I saw something quick scamper and disappear into the brush, something I could not clearly make out. Perhaps a poacher from Vilo-de-la-Mar? I was aware they sometimes hunted in the Riege, but since almost all of them knew me, I must say I rarely frightened them. I checked my horse, cocked my ears, and called into the darkness a few times. No voice replied and, despite my watchfulness, I saw nothing more. And so I thought I had startled some hunter or, although they are quite rare around here, some more suspect wanderer fleeing across the *sansouiro*—a prisoner escaped from the galley-ships in Arles or the jails of Tarascoun. I was very much mistaken in this, as what follows will soon make plain. At the time, however, I did not think much about this false alarm. But Clar-de-Luno, panting and swollen under his straps, did not stop his terrified snorting until we reached the cabin door.

It was just a few days later that, at the northernmost tip of Radèu de l'Aubo, I discovered tracks, *clavo* as we call them in our gardian lingo, that deeply puzzled me when I examined them. Perhaps an untrained eye might take them for the prints of my bulls that frequently crisscross the area. But for a gardian, long accustomed to gauging a bull's weight and age solely by the clavo, the error would be unforgivable. Although cloven like a bull's, these were not a bull's prints, and I could not for an instant be mistaken. These clavo were thinner, longer, and far less deep, especially at the forked tips; moreover, the steps were uneven.

Curious, I followed this track toward the rising sun for something like a half league, but I lost it as I crossed the lagoons, and I was unable to find it again on solid ground. As I needed that day to locate and visit a sick bull roaming on the borders of Badoun, I had to give up my search for the time being.

I did not have to stay away long. The day after the next, I again found similar clavo beside Redoun Lagoon. They skirted the marsh, unequal but quite distinct, clearly visible on the damp sansouiro, stopping, starting, stopping, then finally vanishing into the reed bed. As I had leisure this time, I followed them, and my zeal grew stronger and stronger, for I had come to a conclusion: the animal, I was sure, must be one of those wild boars that haunt the Séuvo and that only rarely venture into the marshes or flats of the sansouiro, whose open vistas displease them. Of course, to judge solely from the size and weight of the claws, this must be a huge animal. But when I left the cabin, I had been careful to bring along my ficheiroun, with the thought, I admit, of perhaps having to fight some wild beast.

I could no longer see the clavo now, but I was determined to make my way down the path the lone creature had opened in the reeds, completely dry at this time of the year. To tell the truth, although the alleyway seemed narrow and small for an animal so heavy and low to the ground, I did my best not to stray from it and to keep on guard. Suddenly, Clar-de-Luno, who can be skittish, swerved for no rhyme or reason—at least as far as I could see—and his hind legs slipped into a mud hole. It took him a huge effort to pull us out, and by the time we were both safely back on more solid ground, the clavo were gone. Because night was already falling at this early hour, I got my bearings, noted my whereabouts, and decided to take up this hunt again as soon as possible—to scour, if need be, all of Redoun Lagoon.

The next day did not go by without my getting back in the saddle. I had made up my mind to find the beast and capture it if I could. Because I wanted first to locate its trails and lair without frightening it—for I was sure that, considering the number of its tracks, it did not want to remain in this area—I did not bring my dog Rasclet but locked him in my cabin in the Riege before leaving. To give myself more time, I ate my breakfast early and filled my satchel with a handful of nuts and dried figs, determined to continue my search until nightfall if need be and to begin again later if I did not succeed.

On that day, the ninth of January, the weather was fine, with a clear sky and a trace of tramontane, the wind from the northern mountains. I had skirted the rim of the lagoons and was heading a little southward on the eastern side. Clar-de-Luno was walking, and, keeping my head down, I was studying the sansouiro in all directions as far as my eyes could see. I even stopped a few times and got off the horse in order to examine more closely some clavo that, mixed in with my bulls' prints, seemed at first glance to mark the beast's passage. But I must say that all morning I found nothing certain.

It was only sometime in the afternoon, around one o'clock, that I actually discovered a fresh track. It came from the Fournelet gaso and went up along Redoun Lagoon. My heart was pounding as I followed it, and I spurred Clar-de-Luno with my legs and heels, making him quicken his pace, for the clavo this time were quite recent: the beast must have passed through here no more than a few hours earlier. When we reached the marsh, it became impossible to follow the tracks for long in the reed bed, where they were soon swallowed up. As on the day before, I focused solely on tracing the path opened by the animal's passage. Yet I had not gone far before I lost it again. Still, seeing that the sun was high for the season and that I had time on my hands, I started to comb through the reeds, going back and forth from east to west and west to east, always watching for mud and quicksand where my horse and I risked being mired.

The tramontane had grown colder and the frost that night promised to be heavy. As I was moving forward into the wind, I had just, without shifting my eyes, turned up my coat's collar and pulled over my ears the winter hood I had made for myself with *vibre* fur. Suddenly Clar-de-Luno leapt to one side, reared back, then planted himself on his four legs, snorting. The reeds were very thick right there, but at that moment I glimpsed—though I could not make it out clearly—something dark and hidden scamper in front of me. I prodded the horse, who took off at a gallop, though he soon stopped short and started to sweat all over, trembling and panting heavily through his nostrils like a basilisk. I could see a wave-like rippling through the reeds a hundred feet away. Annoyed that I had let myself be left behind, I furiously dug my spurs into my horse's flanks, so much so that, with his head down and straining at the bit, he bucked again and again, twisting his haunches in an effort to unseat me. When he saw that he could not succeed, he finally began to walk, trembling under me, trying to regain control and avoid the direction in which I strove to keep him. Not seeing anything move and afraid to lose again the object of my quest, I dug more cruelly with my spurs to make the horse speed up. Clar-de-Luno finally obeyed, but his submission did not last long. He tried to get out from under me, moving sideways and nearly tumbling into a mud hole as he sought to avoid a strange, dark beast crouched in the thickest part of the reed bed.

Halted now, holding my staff aloft, I tried to make out what sort of quarry I had found. I was beginning, I confess, to be alarmed, as my horse's terror—he had never stopped shaking between my legs—was seeping into me.

It was not that the animal looked as dreadful as I had feared. Through the tangled reeds, I barely made out hindquarters covered in coarse, tawny gray hair; I saw two feet with cloven hooves, which I could easily identify. But what stunned me most was glimpsing a sort of rough swaddling cloth plastered to its back and loins. Squatting motionless on its heels, the Beast presented neither its forelegs nor its head. Afraid to startle it if I tried to approach it again and feeling Clar-de-Luno rigid with fear beneath me, ready to put up a fight if I goaded him, I decided to hail this strange creature, to make it turn and look at me. Using no more strength than necessary, I gathered my breath and let out the throaty yell we gardians use to call our bulls when we want to provoke them or to make them stop in their tracks.

"Hè! Hehè! Hè-hehè!"

But I had barely finished my second call before I felt my hair stand on end under my hood and an icy sweat stream down my spine. I had to clutch a handful of mane to keep from fainting—the head turning toward me had a human face!

Despite my terror, I could clearly see strong features carved with suffering and old age, along with wild eyes that burned with a sad flame I found hard to withstand. These details come back to me now, one by one, but at that time I glimpsed them then all at once, as my anxiety mounted.

Until that day, I had never seen anything like it, not in my whole life. Of that I am entirely certain.

But this was nothing compared with what came next. I suddenly felt a wind of abomination blast my face, and I found myself rising straight up in my stirrups, jolted by horror and fear. Because I had just recognized, protruding on each side of the large brow, above the grimy face, two horns. Yes! Two horns, one pathetically broken in the middle, the other half-twisted into a spiral; both rough and stained with mire—the same, I am certain, as those of the goat who haunts the dark and in whose honor they say unhallowed Sabbath masses are celebrated. To save myself, in one swift, instinctive movement, I raised my arm and traced a large sign of the cross in the air. At the same time, I repeated the words of exorcism, just as I had heard my uncle the canon do once when he conjured evil spirits from the body of a possessed woman on the threshold of Nosto-Damo-de-la-Majour.

"*Recede . . . immundissime. Imperat tibi Deus Pater . . . et Filius . . . et Spirtus Sanctus! . . .*"

I was growing stronger, I confess, as I repeated the liturgical formula I had learned as a disciple, and which returned to me now in this pressing danger. To tell the truth, I was expecting to see this vision of Belial dissolve like mist before me, when, to my great amazement, the Beast (what else can I call it?) rose painfully on its stiff legs, and, across its softened features, on its human face, I saw flicker something like a glint of gentleness, the gleam of a melancholy smile.

"Human, do not be alarmed. I am not the devil you dread. You are Christian, I can see that. You are Christian. But I am not a devil . . ."

The Beast was speaking. Its broken, somber voice rang softly, sweetly. Dumbstruck, I listened and felt my fear wane little by little, as a mysterious peace began to flow through my veins. But all of a sudden, I saw the mouth stretch open in a truly diabolic grin, revealing nearly toothless gums. At the same time, a wild laugh rent the air and I had to lower my gaze beneath the creature's blazing, fiery eyes.

"I am not a devil! I am not a devil!"

At that instant the Beast's pupils seemed to fade into mist, and I saw again, shining on its strange face, an ineffably gentle, weary look.

"I am not a devil, and yet you fear me, O human; you make over my face and horns the sign of Christian exorcism. So why do you follow me; why, mounted on your horse and brandishing your three-pointed spear, do you hunt me? Tell me, why do you follow me? What have I done to you? This land is the last where I have found some peace and the sacred solitude where once I exerted my youthful strength, when I reigned, master of silence and the hours, master of the infinite song that rises starward from the insects of the plain, spreading through the hollows of the deep. Here, amid these salt flats broken by lagoons and sandy beaches, listening to your bulls' bellows and wild stallions' neighs—hidden by day to watch veils of mirage sway above the burning sansouiro and by night to see the bright, bare moon dance above the sea—I have known moments that, for me, can be called happy. Yes, happy. Why do you stare at me like that, your eyes wide open and your face whiter than if you were about to die just to see me? Shattered as I am, lame and conquered, I was happy on this barren land that barely provides what I need to sustain my ancient body, but which grants me the wild wind I cannot live without, and for which I abandoned the sweet meadows, flowering gardens, and warm beaches where, night and day, the sea breathes and swells like the rise and fall of a young breast. Poor human. And here it is that, panting, you chase and follow me for several days, you arm yourself to fight me, you hunt me down like a wild beast whose forlorn pelt you long to win. Are my peace and poor happiness over simply because, tonight, a human looks upon me face to face? Come, tell me. What do you want from me?"

Numb with fear, I was standing stock-still on my horse. My teeth were clattering. My lips were tightly clenched, and in my mouth my dead tongue felt rough and coarse, like a block of wood.

Night was falling. The west was reddish, its flames spreading eastward as if stoked by the mistral. The piercing wind, now colder and harsher, had turned my clothes—soaked with the anxious sweat endlessly streaming down my skin—into a heavy cloak of ice.

I could not tear my eyes away from the mysterious face reddening in the glow of dusk. A gleam crowned the brow, setting the eyes ablaze, lengthening the horns' awful shadow through the reeds. Unable to say a word, I somehow managed to straighten up. I took Clar-de-Luno well in hand, quickly traced from my head to my shoulders another large sign of the cross to dispel these dreadful illusions, turned around, and, without looking back, without slowing down, raced to my cabin door. How I managed to dismount and unsaddle the horse, how, after gulping down some water, I undressed and fell onto my bunk, comes back to me now in a fog. All I know for certain is that I had nightmares all night long; I could not stop moaning and shivering, as if suddenly gripped by one of those marsh fevers.

Indeed, I remained dazed and beaten for several days, like someone emerging from illness. I rose in the morning, my legs limp, my head heavy, my stomach churning. I roamed the cabin, too weak to do a thing, driven mad by ghastly visions that had hounded me all night in dreams. Although my burning lips and throat made me swallow huge mouthfuls of water at every turn, I had no taste for food.

I was so sick that, to replace myself at work, I briefly thought about calling on my older brother Louvis, nicknamed *Bon-Pache*, who herds at Clamadou on the other side of the Little Rhône. But my certainty that nothing could endanger the manado, coupled with the unshakable reluctance I suddenly felt about letting anyone else learn of such an awful mystery, kept me, I admit, from putting this plan into action. I decided I would summon him only if events forced me to. No doubt the fear of reaching that point very much speeded my recovery.

For a long time, I was possessed by a true madness whose back-and-forth battering wore me to the bone. More than once, I would have felt I was truly losing my mind if I had not turned to the prayers that, I confess, I neglect too much in the lonely life I lead here by our lagoons. And so I would cross myself, and, closing my eyes, begin to pray. But right in the middle of the Our Father, I would suddenly stop, seeing within myself the horns and ravaged brow, hearing the appalling laugh. I cannot express the horror I felt as I relived my encounter in the reeds. And yet—and here is what truly tortured me—a desire, deep down, was eating away at me. A burning desire to know, to know more, was attracting me to the hideous creature, half beast or half devil—who knows?—from which I had fled as I felt my soul reel.

And so, day and night, one way or another, I was constantly possessed by the same terror. Yes, possessed; I tremble as I write this terrible word; how often have I not warded off with an invocation the horrid phantom that was hounding me?

Another thought was haunting me and making my anxiety grow. How, when I studied the clavo that first day, had I not seen that they followed one another like a man's, instead of like the four prints a wild boar's hooves—or the hooves of any other ordinary animal—would have made?

I told myself, first, that I had almost never been able to observe those clavo except when they were broken up and mixed in with other tracks; second—as I had noticed more than once—among some animals with an ambling gait, the rear clavo often covers the front; and, finally, not expecting anything so strange and unforeseen, I had chosen, without much thought, the simplest explanation. But in my feverish state this answer hardly satisfied me, and I was convinced that my very confusion stemmed from some illusion that smacked of sorcery.

I hardly went out, neglecting my animals and always seeing before me—no matter what I did—this thing I would now have been pained to learn had completely disappeared, yet which I dreaded actually meeting again. This dread, I must admit, dominated me. I felt that if the Beast were suddenly to appear before me, I would not be able to face it without swooning. The Beast? I was sure I was not at all dealing with any animal to be found in nature. But still, how could I take it for a devil? Twice I had traced the Christian sign above it in the air; twice I had pronounced the holy words that, everyone knows, evil spirits cannot withstand. And twice had I not seen it, with its cloven hooves and two horns, unmoved by prayers and the sign said to bring unbearable suffering to devils and the damned? Had I not seen it standing still, like a stone? Had I not seen it also smile? And so? How to know, when, above all, a blinding fear kept me bound hand and foot?

After a few days, though, nature won out. I felt like eating again, and, as my stomach gained strength, a bit of courage also returned.

It was a good two weeks after the events at Redoun Lagoon I have just described, when, feeling stronger, I decided to resume my work and go out in search of a cow I had not seen for a while and which by my reckoning must be on the verge of calving. I must confess I had to force myself to place my foot in the stirrup and to hoist myself into the saddle that day. Anxiety stiffened my legs and weighed down my whole body. I have already noted the determination that, on the other hand, drove me to conquer my fear.

And so I headed with small steps toward the Enforo, the Outskirts, where I hoped to find the group of cows, but I was careful to avoid the tip of Redoun Lagoon. I rode along without the courage to look around; when I noticed groups of very fresh clavo on the ground, I turned my head and made sure not to stop. You have to have known my weakness and to have felt my terror to understand such faintheartedness. But I write only to report the truth. I was afraid.

Around midday, I finally found my cow at rest in the shade of some junipers. She was already caring for a small black calf with soft fur. Absorbed in suckling when it heard my horse's muffled step on the sand, it turned a frizzy head, its muzzle dripping milk. The nursing mother fixed me with a fierce eye and began to toss her head and scratch the sand with her hoof, warning me that my visit angered her and that, to protect her little one, she was ready to charge. I moved away then, as would anyone in my place, satisfied that I had completed my task and done my gardian's duty. Yet I was also secretly pleased not to have met anything along the way that might suggest the Beast's presence, whether near or far. The memory of that creature, the mere thought of it, haunted me; day by day it grew more and more unbearable. I tried to persuade myself, without much conviction, that I had suffered some kind of hallucination, that the vision I saw once would most likely not be repeated. But to tell the truth, my mind was sorely troubled by this strange shock. Deep down, I was burning to discover what would come out of all this and what would finally explain the mystery I did not yet have the courage to face.

Little by little I took up my life and my usual habits. I came and went as before. I hunted. In the evening I laid rabbit and duck snares to trap game and keep hunger at bay. I rode horseback; and each morning as before, I saddled Clar-de-Luno and crisscrossed the land to find my bulls and drive them back within bounds.

Some time after the astonishing encounter of the day I will never forget even if I were to live a thousand years, but about which I forced myself to think as little as possible, I roped in a young colt on the manado. Everyone knows how these things are done. As he went by, I used my horsehair *seden* to lasso the *quatren* I liked the most and whom I judged best suited to bear a saddle and make a good mount. But our Camargue horses are quite wild, with a temper that makes them hard to control. In his terror, this one turned out to be so headstrong and excitable that, after letting him freely rear and buck at the end of the rope, I held on with all my might and then let myself go, lying full length on the sand, now pulled and dragged along, now arching back and digging my toes into the sansouiro, until he finally collapsed, legs folded under him, neck stretched out, throat held so tightly in the noose he could barely breathe. That's when I rushed to his side, threw a halter over his head, and—as he was three-quarters strangled—loosened the seden's knot so he could catch his breath.

It is common knowledge that gardians typically work in pairs to break in young horses. But I was set on taming this one without anyone's help— strange feeling that possessed me and which I could not overcome. I have already said it: I felt then, as I still do today, an unspeakable horror at the thought that the abomination I had seen might be made known to anyone else. And so I decided to break in Vibre all by myself. That was the name I gave him on the spot, at first because of his coat's color, but which I mean for him to keep. Later that first evening I tethered him to a post behind my cabin and brought him one of the sheaves of dry reeds I reap yearly during good weather and put aside to feed my riding horses in winter. The next day, I shortened his rope, gently blinkered his eyes, and immobilized one of his hind legs by lifting it with a rope, using a special knot we call an *ausso-pèd*. Despite his snorts, shivers, sweats, and other contortions common to wild colts, I went to work to put a saddle on his back, to accustom him to the weight of a harness. Next, I unblinkered his eyes, released his foot, and began to lead him, all puffed up and rigid with fear under his straps. I went on foot, holding him firmly and letting him walk at my pace. I made no sudden movements and did not shout; instead I reasoned with him in a gentle, hushed voice as I pulled him from the front. So as not to anger him, I was careful not to turn back and look him in the eye.

After several days of this handling, wild as he was, he had grown tame enough for me to think about having him walk another way. So I got in the saddle on Clar-de-Luno as usual, and, each morning as I rounded up my bulls, I led Vibre gently by his tether, making him follow me as I walked, trotted, or galloped. When gardians work in pairs to break in a new horse, they never go to so much trouble. But I had to be very cautious with this animal I knew was restive and rebellious, aware that the least upset would make me lose the little territory I seemed to have gained. Moreover, since I was alone, I feared that an accident might leave me in a difficult position.

And so, as soon as I found him docile enough, I was careful to wear him out before having him submit to the weight and control of a horseman. I led him *en dèstre* at the end of the seden beside Clar-de-Luno, sometimes making him gallop and sometimes restraining him, then taking off in a zigzag and clucking my tongue to accustom him to commands.

I returned from the Enforo around ten o'clock that morning. In the saddle for some three hours already, I immediately sat down to eat. I had decided to mount Vibre for the first time, and so I ate quickly, just a slice of cold rabbit grilled on the hearth the night before. I rounded out my meal with a few nuts and dried figs, slipping a handful into my pocket along with a crust of bread, as I do when work forces me to eat early and I do not know when I will be back. To quench my thirst, I drank only some water drawn from the jug where I collect it. But as I was getting up from the table, I took down from the shelf the bottle of sweet liqueur made by the monks at the Abbey, which the Father Abbot had sent me at New Year's. I uncorked it and swallowed just one mouthful as my stirrup cup.

I record all these details one by one, knowing full well they will one day seem tiresome and dull. But I believe I must firmly establish that no one should here suspect either the fantasies of fever or the delusions of drunkenness. What is more, I do not write, I repeat, for the idle amusement of whoever might one day read me, but rather to communicate these bewildering experiences to others more equipped than I to understand and explain them. I write, more than anything, to unburden myself.

We had just then reached the twelfth of February and so were entering the season when the evening's light begins to last a little longer. The wind, which had blown from the north for some time, was calm now, and the sky was limpid and clear, from the east all the way to the *largado*. Around midday, I went to untie Vibre, on whose back I had been careful to leave the saddle since early morning. After attentively and firmly tightening the straps, I placed a good *cabassoun* with horsehair reins over his nose, and in his mouth the bridle bit I always used for young horses. It had been forged for me by a blacksmith in Lunèu, and I like it because it is both gentle and firm, crafted to spare the mouth of a new animal yet able to keep it in check if it tries to break free. Horsemen, if any happen to read this, will readily understand me. I led Vibre on foot at an easy pace until we reached the sandy strip along the margin of the radèu. I wanted to mount him somewhere with no trees in the way. When I reached the spot, I checked the straps and the whole harness again, soothing Vibre with a whistle, but without touching him, because our Camargue horses do not like to be patted. I blinkered his eye with the side of my hand, then placed my foot in the stirrup and hoisted myself into the saddle as gently as I could. I did not have to hang on tight; after hesitating a moment and turning in place, Vibre set off without balking, at that faltering gait young horses use when they walk between a man's legs for the first time.

We plodded at that pace for about an hour. Vibre went along, tossing his neck between the reins, panting with fear, looking anxious and sullen, but soon he seemed to accept his new position. I was careful to skirt the radèu along their margins, keeping to my right the thicket and to my left the bare expanse, still flooded at this time of year. Suddenly, with that abrupt violence common among our Camargue horses, Vibre caught me off guard. With no warning, he brought his muzzle down between his forelegs and began to buck with great kicks, sometimes plunging forward and sometimes twisting backward, snorting and neighing the whole time. I was so surprised by this behavior that, despite all my efforts, I could not raise up the bedeviled head that pulled and weighed more than a hundred kilos at the end of my arms. Slowly but surely shaken by the repeated shocks of this beast that bucked and reared at each step with increasing violence, I could no longer stay in the saddle. Tossed from the horse, I found myself roughly hurled against the foot of a juniper, then rolled onto the sand, where I lay, just about completely dazed. But not so much so as not to glimpse, as in a nightmare, the freed Vibre, his tail straight out and his muzzle to the wind, galloping wildly toward the manado.

I must have lain like that, as if dead, for several hours. When I came to, I felt my dog Rasclet gently licking my face. The sun was already low and the wind on the lagoons was blowing briskly. To my relief, as you can imagine, I found that my only wound—aside from some bruises to the rest of my body—was a scrape on my ear, where the blood was already drying. My head heavy and my legs stiff, I rose. Unable just then to wreak vengeance on the animal, I confined myself to cursing him with the worst insults, roundly blasting his father, his bitch of a mother, and her entire bloodline. My mouth was ablaze, but I never blasphemed the Holy Names, which—unlike most gardians—I respect even in my greatest rages.

I immediately set out for my cabin, choosing the shortest path through the radèu, sure that I would find Vibre among the manado's mares, but anxious about my bridle and harness as a result of this mishap.

To tell the truth, even as I limped along, dragging my bruised leg through the brush, I could not ward off a very strong concern: Would this animal, who seemed so naturally rebellious and who had once unseated me, become unapproachable? And how, if he were to unseat me again, would I afterwards tame him with no help? Yet I was convinced I had to capture him anew and dominate him right away if possible, because everyone knows how wild new horses become when they get the better of you at the first try and you do not master them immediately.

And so, lost in thought, I was turning all this over in my mind as I neared my cabin. I was less than half a league away when my dog Rasclet, who had been sniffing around a bush, suddenly withdrew and whimpered in terror. He was in such a rush to hide that he almost knocked me down as he roughly thrust his muzzle between my legs. When I bent over to see what was causing such terror, I saw before me—him or her, I do not know—the Beast, squatting on the ground and digging in the sand at the foot of a juniper.

My first impulse was to jump back and flee without a fight. For its part, the Beast rose up, like a timid creature frightened by the sight of man, and dependent solely on its own speed for safety. But when it recognized me, it seemed suddenly reassured: its cheeks creased, its mouth opened, and its bitter, cackling laugh rang through the woods like the screech of a monstrous cicada.

"Perhaps you would rather run away, strange man who seeks me and who, as soon as you hear my voice, flees, as if the north wind carried you off. Tell me, what have you done today with your iron and your horse, and why are you dragging your leg like that?"

Surprise, I must admit, had sealed my lips. This sudden meeting, just when I was absorbed in other thoughts and anxieties, had rattled me. I could not say a word in reply. While the creature was speaking, my dog Rasclet, at first hiding next to me, had started slowly creeping toward the Beast. (So that I can be understood here, I will keep this name for the creature.) As he moved closer, Rasclet whimpered; then, seemingly spellbound, he lay flat on the ground, his muzzle stretched forward. Despite my shock, I could not help but notice him. But the Beast was no longer laughing. It had sat down, leaning on one of its elbows. I was disturbed by the sight of the mangy fleece flecking its goat legs and the dull, scaly cloven hooves, with their filthy, curved tips.

"You are still here, staring at me," it continued, "and I question you as if you were not a limited human. I question you, and you do not even know why you live on this barren plain, encircled as far as the eye can see by the sea's vast sweep and the Cévennes' blue haze. What do you know? Nothing. What do you do? Not much, yet something nobler and higher, perhaps, than you can fathom. Unwittingly, you perpetuate rites that are among humankind's most venerable, and by instinct you repeat actions whose greatness you cannot measure. And yet, as you look upon my poverty-stricken old age, you have no notion what the youth of a demigod might be."

"Blasphemy!" I cried as I leapt back, chilled by a blast of horror. "Blasphemy and sacrilege! There can be no demigods. There is but one God, one eternal God who created heaven and earth—in the Name of the Father, the Son, and the Holy Ghost."

"You speak rightly," the Beast replied, without showing any feeling this time, "you speak rightly. There is but one eternal God. Once, wandering on Libya's borders centuries ago, already seeking desert air and free light, I chanced upon a man who seemed about a hundred years old, as wild as I. He lived alone in the vastness, depriving himself, as a sacrifice, of all he could. He announced what he called the Good News and taught me words that, like a blazing flame, lit up the dark whirlpool of my blood's proud waves. There is but one eternal God. But there were once gods, gods born from the earth and who, upon the earth, are now dead. There are demigods. You cannot perhaps truly understand that. There are demigods. They live a sovereign life, slaked by floats of ether, drunk on earthly essences. Masters of a world in flower, spun in the dance of seasons and stars, they sing with the same voice as sunlight and sea. Ah! If you could have seen me then— me!—when, proud and free, bursting with youthful vigor, I leapt at noon through clearings, frightening solely by my presence the woodland creatures I enjoyed outrunning; or when, crouched in mist during the sweet nighttime hours, keen with cunning and desire, I spied, to surprise and seize them, shapes so lovely that, as I see them again, even from this distance, I can scarcely call them bodies. Look at me. With these horns on my head and my animal hooves, can you ignore the signs? Do you take me for a man? There is but one eternal God. But demigods are born, live, and grow old; and, after a life your reason could not reckon without losing itself, they die; yes, they die, returning to the gulfs of space and time, and, as for me, I do not know where they are led by the will that once brought them forth."

I was still listening attentively, straining to engrave in memory so many words I did not fully understand. The other, the Beast, silent for a long time, not looking at me, seemed lost in thought.

"Demigods live. Or rather, I should say, they lived. Because, in all the time I have been wandering this immense earth, now feeling myself grow old and watching the world's splendor dim before my eyes, falling to pieces, it has been very long since I have had the least encounter with my own kind. Perhaps, like me, they are hiding, afraid in this age of men's barbarity and malice. Think what you yourself experienced when you first saw me.

"In the old days the sight of us always caused panic. In jest, how often have I not hidden behind bushes in the heart of a vast countryside and suddenly rushed out crying, delighted to see herders and their herds vanish in mad flight across the plain? But although men feared us then, they also honored us. How many suns upon suns have passed since I have seen young demigods leap in summer streams, lighter than young goats!

"One time, the last—so long ago!—while out hunting at night I saw a white shape slip through a copse. I was longing to caress her female lips.

I ran, caught her in my arms, drew her from shadow into moonlight. She looked at me and, making no effort to free herself, began to smile sadly. Alas! Her sweet cheeks were wrinkled; her mouth no longer had teeth; and in the wells of her eyes, I clearly saw that love had forever gone dry. I released her, let her go without a word. She was indeed the last, yes, the last I met since then."

I did not breathe a word, struck dumb by all I had heard. I turned my eyes away from the strange, now silent mouth; I looked at Rasclet, still stretched out as if prostrate before the Beast, emitting what sounded like affectionate whimpers from time to time. It was then that my gaze was arrested by a hole at most two handspans wide, dug into the dirt and next to which I saw some freshly pulled-up roots.

"Yes, demigods are not only born and live, but, unless they are to die, they also must eat. What do you expect me to do? How could I prowl around villages and farms without being hounded like a plundering beast? And then, haven't I told you? As much as food for my body, I need free air and wild sky. And on this desert land, I maintain my old bones as best I can. As you see, when you surprised me this time without meaning to, I was digging up some roots that seem good when there is nothing better to sink your teeth into. But soon fresh asparagus shoots will spring up around the thickets; and then there are partridge eggs, along with the eggs of seabirds and flamingos; there are heron and teal nests. It is not much. What do you expect? It is as if the earth, since it first began to spin, no longer seems made for us."

He was speaking now in a muffled voice, as if stricken. And his resigned face no longer bore a trace of bitterness. For the first time I noticed his shoulders—sunburnt and black, but so thin, so thin that at the least movement I could see the bones of each joint moving back and forth. As I gazed at his drawn features and worn body—half-divine as he claimed—feeding, famished, on a poor handful of roots, I was moved by a great pity. In an instant I forgot my first horror, the monstrousness of the beast-like brow and cloven hooves. I thrust my hand into my jacket pocket and drew out the bread, nuts, and dried figs I had brought with me that morning, just in case. At the sight of this meager meal, the dull eyes revived.

"Here!" I said, reaching my hand out to him.

He took a step, hesitated, his two hands open. I saw that they were long and thin, tense, with sharp nails at the fingertips.

I quickly poured in all I held in mine.

"Are you hungry?"

But I heard no voice. The two palms filled with bread and fruit were crossed on the emaciated chest. The hands were avidly clenched, as if clutching precious prey. As I retook my path, I saw, when I turned back to whistle for my dog, the old face stretching toward me with an ineffable look of rapture and ecstasy, as two large tears suddenly fell from the blinking eyelids and flowed silently through the gray beard.

The next few days were, for me, filled with torment and trouble. As I thought back to all that had happened, I could not entirely ward off the suspicion of some diabolic spell, despite the futility of exorcisms and signs of the cross. But on the other hand, as I recalled the creature's reasoning, and, above all, as I saw again the fleeting sweetness of its face and the pride of what might be its soul; when I remembered how filled with thanks it was for the little gift I offered—I let my first fear be followed by compassion, and I felt a kind of friendship develop in me. That was what, day and night now, I could not help thinking about. At night especially, as I feverishly tossed and turned, I swung from one feeling to the next, now repulsed in horror and fear, now giving way to a weakness I did not understand.

This struggle poisoned my sleep and plagued my dreams. Even as I went about my work, I could not stop thinking about the Beast. I was haunted as much inside my cabin when I made my bed and prepared my meals as outdoors when I rounded up my beasts for the night or crossed the vast Enforo of the Riege in the early morning.

You need to know the Camargue and to have led a gardian's life to understand how a single thought can possess a man's soul when, with no answering voice and attended only by his dreams, he rides alone on horseback through the sansouiro, like a ship a-sail on a desert sea.

Which is why I did as little as possible, devoting myself to a task that could best distract me from my worries. I had found Vibre again, quite calm among the mares and with my saddle, luckily, still intact. He was easy enough to handle. I did not have to lasso him with the seden but simply used some tricks to catch him by the cabassoun's reins, which he was dragging along on the ground. I brought him back and tethered him again behind my cabin, determined to mount him as soon as I could; otherwise, I was sure he would become more and more unapproachable.

But before that, I had to go to Vilo-de-la-Mar. That's where the Father Abbott sends me supplies every fortnight with one of the Abbey's carters. I went as usual on Clar-de-Luno, leading along Pavoun, a worn-out old horse that, when I need to, I make bear, like a real pack animal, the *ensàrri*, those large baskets that hang over an animal's sides and are so good for carrying all sorts of things.

I returned in the evening without visiting anyone other than our venerable priest. He thought my face looked ill and my eye fevered; I blamed it on marsh sickness. When he gently reproached me for having too long neglected my Christian duties, I reassured him and led him to believe I had performed them recently at the Abbey. I cannot say how much such a lie now pains me. I do not count as a visit dropping by to say hello to Touniet, a sea fisherman, my comrade, who has always been a friend. He too thought I looked peaked, and he urged me to drink an infusion of centaury for a few days. He refused to let me leave before handing me two fine Saint Peter fish, in thanks for some wildfowl I had brought him. Before returning to the cabin, I stopped at the barber's, whose day it was, to have my long, bristly beard trimmed—and also to learn whether anything had been breathed about the strange Beast haunting the Vacarés, here in this spot where gardians and poachers gather to trade the gossip and tall tales of the Camargue. On this point, I was completely reassured.

The sun was just setting when I already found myself back at my cabin. I immediately began to put away all the supplies I had brought back. I was pleased to find a little sack of figs, another of nuts and sweet almonds, along with two dozen mountain apples, somewhat wrinkled by winter, but still crisp and sweet under their tough red skins. For dinner, I cooked the fish my comrade had given me and set aside a portion for my breakfast.

The next day, before mounting Clar-de-Luno, I took a feedbag, of the sort we call a *saquetoun*. I filled it with a good helping of dried fruit and half a loaf of bread; then I added a piece of fish and two fine apples.

As I made my way toward the Enforo, I took a detour to pass by the juniper at whose foot I had last met the Beast; I hung the saquetoun from one of its highest branches, safe from foxes, birds of prey, or other pests. To be even safer, I tied the canvas shut with a reed knot. When I returned in the evening, I saw it had not been touched, and I promised myself to check it again once the night was over.

The next day, I rose before dawn. To dress, I had to give myself some light with my *calèu*. It was calm and cold out and the sky was still dark when I opened my door. I was hurrying. I had already gulped down my hot soup by the time my fire was ablaze and the dawn's first gleams were beginning to redden earth and water. I was all set, ready to remount Vibre, but not without taking as best I could all the necessary precautions so that this time I would remain master. I saddled him with the same care and attention as before, and, to tire him a bit, first used the seden to lead him at a trot while I rode Clar-de-Luno. He walked beside me, a little behind, his head down and his eye drooping, like an animal coming to terms with having a weight on his back, and who, henceforth, would no longer be frightened by either the creak of leather or the clank of metal.

That day I let the bulls do as they pleased, so that I could devote all my time to this training, whose outcome, I must say, worried me. I led Vibre through the woods, making him walk through the brush behind Clar-de-Luno to accustom him to twigs scratching around the saddle; but I was also anxious to learn whether the Beast had found the food I had hung for it from the juniper's highest branch. When I reached the spot and dismounted, I saw that the saquetoun had been emptied and closed again, as if by a man's hand. At the base of the tree, I noticed a trail of clavo I had not seen before, although I had taken care, in the evening, to smooth the entire surface of the ground with my hands. I took down the saquetoun and was surprised to discover that something remained. It was the piece of fish I had put in with the other supplies. When I thought about it, I concluded that the Beast must be repulsed by animal flesh, and that, in this way, it wanted to let me know. Later events only confirmed this suspicion.

I returned to my cabin to eat, and I finished so quickly that when I was ready to take Vibre again, the sun barely marked eight o'clock. The sky, as I have noted, was calm and clear. And, despite the anxiety that never stopped tormenting me, I felt that lightness of body granted by good weather, especially at this time of year when new life is surging up beneath the waning winter.

I led Vibre into an open area, where I had him take a few steps. Then I blinkered him and placed my foot in the stirrup to hoist myself into the saddle. The animal did not bolt but set off calmly at a halting yet gentle pace. I let him continue like this for almost a league. If we had not had our earlier mishap, I might have dozed off, convinced I was safe. But I knew only too well what he was like deep down, and, not wanting to be surprised, I remained on guard against any caprice. This care proved unnecessary. I made him walk for two hours or so. I knew that too much tiredness could enrage him, and I did not want to overdo it with an animal that had been free for so long. Still, I focused on breaking his strength by deliberately leading him through mud and sand and letting him struggle as much as he could. But soon I found myself back near my cabin without Vibre having attempted the slightest leap or shown any sign of ill will. I watered him right away, tossed him a few good sheaves of dry reeds, and then, famished myself, quickly made a meal of some bitter olives and a chunk of fresh Tomme cheese I had brought back from Vilo-de-la-Mar.

Night did not fall without my having bridled and mounted Vibre again. I went along as I had earlier for at most an hour and then I let him rest before unsaddling him, simply wanting to have him feel my weight and mastery. My plan was to not interrupt this training, no matter what, without first pushing him fairly far.

I resumed the task the next day and every morning thereafter when I had the time. We were then at the beginning of March. Although nights and mornings were still cool, the daytime sun was starting to heat things up. Already the approaching spring could be sensed through more than one sign of the new season. A green sap was rising through the thin tamarisk shoots; fresh reeds were poking up from the water in the marsh, and, in the early morning, you could hear all the little birds calling each other along the shore. This was a little more than a month ago, as it was on Holy Easter Sunday—the eleventh of April, exactly sixteen days ago now—that I began to write in this journal. Today, spring's joy is bursting everywhere. But in early March, after a hard winter, it could barely be glimpsed.

I left that day without neglecting my usual precautions and without trusting my mount's seeming submission. As on the day before, I began my circuit along the edge of the radèu. The horse was already moving with a firmer step and I could feel his mouth responding more readily to the pressure of the bit. Quitting the open border, I undertook to lead him into the thicket, just in case keeping him on the better-worn paths through the woods where I had led him earlier behind Clar-de-Luno. I had made him take the first turn without a hitch when I suddenly felt him puff up between my knees, bucking furiously, his back arched and his head between his legs, *se desbrandant* as we say, and whinnying furiously. I clung to the cantle, hanging on for dear life, as I knew only too well what would happen if I let myself be unsaddled again. I could feel the bucks coming hard and fast, one after another, as if I were being tossed on a sea swell, and I sensed the moment coming when I would have no choice but to capsize.

That was when something remarkable happened. Just as he was plunging forward, Vibre fell back down and stood stiffly on his four legs, as if his hooves were planted in the earth. His whinnies and snorts stopped, and he remained rigid under me, as if turned to stone. At the same time, I saw the Beast. It too was standing still, leaning against a juniper trunk, its blazing eyes fixed on my horse. It was blowing gently through its lips, whistling. Then it began to sway on its legs, moving forward with small steps as if dancing, still whistling and gazing deeply at Vibre, gradually whistling louder and moving faster. When it was right beside me, not more than two feet from my horse's head, I could feel the horse, still planted under me, begin to shudder with a subtle, inward tremor, the way water suddenly starts to stir when touched by a flame's heat.

But the other, having come forward, stopped, suspended its strange song, raised its arm, and firmly laid the palm of its open hand on Vibre's brow. The horse, usually so quick to take fright at the least gesture, saw it coming, but reacted no more than would a stone. And once the hand was set between his ears, he began to tremble without moving his feet, shaking all over between my legs and groaning in pain, like a bound animal on whose living flesh you plant a red-hot brand. Then, slowly and shakily, he began to fold his limbs, first the forelegs, then the hindlegs, continuing to shiver and pant, until—with me still on him—he was completely laid low on the ground. But just as he touched the earth, the Beast suddenly withdrew, and Vibre, released, rose at once and stood upright on his legs, as if possessed by a heavy, sad stupor, his skin quivering and covered in froth.

At this sight, the strange creature burst out laughing and screeched—I have already noted this trait—like a monstrous cicada whose song causes the whole forest to shudder.

"You can mount him now, he will be tame. You can ride him without fear of being rolled in the mud like a swamp eel or tossed in the air like a gull. It is true that demigods frighten herders, but they also know how to tame wild animals. You have seen it. Do you still take me for a beast? No, after all," the creature continued, letting its features soften and lifting from its face the scowl that made it look so dreadful. "No, I know you are a better man than most. Did you not conquer your fear and the sacred horror that, without meaning to, I inspire in you? What is more, did you hesitate to give up some of your own food to ease my hunger, even though I did not ask for it?"

I was looking and listening silently, sensing Vibre still frozen and numb. As for me, I was stunned, deeply troubled to see that this force, surely supernatural, had felled such a wayward beast.

"Do not be afraid any longer," said the being, whom I could no longer call the Beast. "I am not one of those evil spirits, filthy larvae the old hermit in Libya exorcised before my eyes. What I am, you perhaps already know and will perhaps always deny. I have accepted the eternal God. I have sung with all the voices of the world. I have followed, with my dance, the revolutions of the stars. And here, now, I feel my ancient flesh shriveling under my skin like the wood of an old tree that can no longer suck life from the dried-up sap beneath its bark. The times have turned, I know, and my reign is already over. But I will maintain my power until the very end, I will master the beasts of the plain and the wild animals of the woods. I will know how to make them bow and submit. So, go, do what you will with your horse. I have tamed him forever for you; do not forget that this hand has touched him."

And then I spurred Vibre. He turned and began to walk at my command. As I went, I looked back at the other one. He was gazing at me. Never before had I seen him look so proud, so aglow. Before I left, I hesitated a moment, and I cannot keep myself now from recalling the smile of pleasure and peace that seemed just then to light up the ancient face.

This is what I saw. This is what I anxiously write here. Will those who one day read me have complete faith in my tale? Should they think me the victim of a brain fever, let them ponder whether my madness could at the same time derange the animals around me. I know that sick dreams might have given rise to the kinds of visions I have painted. I myself have sometimes thought that a fever's fantasy made me believe that, mounted on Vibre, I met the Beast and took part in the miraculous events I have reported. But precisely, and to speak only of Vibre, it must be taken into account that, ever since then, I saddle and mount him daily, I make him turn and leap at my whim, I lead him wherever I please. This fact, day after day, cannot truly be a dream. Never again has the animal offered the least resistance to my commands. Even more astonishing, and something I have never before witnessed: when he is running freely with the other animals and I want to catch him, I do not have to lure him with a saquetoun full of oats or to seize him by surprise and encircle him with a lasso as in the past. The minute he sees me, he stops, his head turned toward me, calmly waiting for me to slip the double cord of my seden around his neck. Such behavior by one of our Camargue horses, until now completely free, will, I am sure, amaze anyone who knows the natural wildness and fitfulness of this breed. Ever since that day, he lets me saddle and bridle him with more ease than the other riding horses, and I mount him with no preparation or precaution, with no more risk than if, having removed the ensàrri from his back, I had the crazy notion of straddling old Pavoun.

This is what I have seen, what I have felt, what I know. This also is what torments and assails me. I reaffirm that I possess all my faculties, but if this trouble continues, I do not know how it will all end.

Of course, the mere existence of the Beast and its presence here could be taken, in and of themselves, as great miracles. I was already beginning to accept them. Although at first they were the dread cause of my torments, these torments were beginning to lessen, bit by bit. But ever since with my own eyes, I saw its power manifest, ever since I was witness to the amazing feat, to which I would not know how to give another name without blasphemy, I feel my anxieties reborn.

As I was bringing the tamed Vibre back from the radèu, all I felt was great gratitude. I was thinking only of the danger averted and the service rendered. Now I have thought it over some more. Despite everything he told me, do I know, with the little information I have, what this being is? Do I know, after all, what most of his words really mean, even though each time I force myself to preserve them precisely in my head in order to write them down? How can I be certain they do not contain some dreadful spell? Should I not remember the revulsion I felt at first, and mistrust this odd affection, this strange friendship that, little by little, like a charm, casts a spell on my heart? I do not know; how can I know? And I do not know, finally, if all this can happen without endangering my soul—even though, for some time now, I have fervently resumed my prayers and endlessly entrust myself to my patron saints. Yet here it is that I have let Easter go by without daring to approach the confessional. Speak of all this? Never. Just as much as on the first day, it would be impossible. And I do not dare to partake of the Sacrament without confessing to the Father what now possesses me.

Although I continue to cross and recross the Riege, the Enforo, and Redoun Lagoon, the Beast has not appeared to me since the day it tamed Vibre. It has already been quite some time. Just as it arrived, so perhaps it has left to seek another refuge, granting my soul the right to reclaim its solitude and peace. I write this with a feeling of sorrow and remorse I alone can comprehend.

For a long while now, I have seen nothing more. Nowhere have I been able to find fresh clavo. So there could be no doubt, I hung from the high branch of the juniper the saquetoun filled with nuts and dried figs. No one, this time, has untied the knot. The Beast has gone I think, but my trouble remains. I wish, I regret, and also I fear; above all, I fear.

Ever since that dreadful day when it appeared to me for the first time in the middle of the marsh, my soul retains an image that will haunt me until I take my last breath. This is how things stand. My brain is now like the blazing beach where the August sun stirs its great mirages.

What to believe? Ever since the rays from its eyes burned mine, the image of reality within me is a distorted, dancing glimmer.

Out loud, to be sure, I will say nothing. It is enough to write to unburden myself, as much as possible, of this crushing weight. That is why I have tried to record very faithfully what I have seen and all the events in which I have taken part until this very hour.

Here is what I now believe: The Beast is gone. Until today, I have searched, and I have seen nothing, nothing more. If nothing remarkable happens later, this is where my tale ends, for all time. Let no one reproach me. However poor and tangled it seems, it has brought me, in my trouble, unspeakable relief.

I do not flatter myself that I have been able, in this way, to dispel all that haunts me.

Yet I am comforted to think that the wondrous events that troubled a poor gardian in his solitude will not be swallowed in the abyss of time, lost like so many others, and that one day someone wiser and more learned than I will come and, observing them from afar without terror, will know how to explain and understand what my ignorance alone perhaps veils from me today.

Second Chapter

Everything I saw before was nothing.

All the wondrous events I recounted above, since my first meeting with the Beast, could pass as common and customary, compared with those that have come to me since.

And so I take up this notebook again to record once more what I feel must be recorded.

It has been some three months since I have written anything. I thought this story was over and done with. At first, five weeks that could not have been more peaceful went by. Not that I could fully put to rest my memory of those strange events, which, no matter what I did, still haunted me. But despite all my searching and all my vigilance, I could not find any fresh clavo—other than those of my animals—in the countryside. The saquetoun, which I still visited from time to time, hung from the same branch, untouched for days on end, still tied shut and filled with delicacies.

I told myself that the unknown being whom I had called the Beast must have left the area, that milder weather and plentiful fruit allowed it to find food much more easily elsewhere. Although this mystery more or less completely filled my mind, I tried to think about it as little as possible.

In order to free myself once and for all, I thought at first to no longer hang the saquetoun, to forgo this offering that had grown useless, serving solely to prolong my agony. But one morning as I was completing my usual rounds, I noticed that the saquetoun was wide open, its reed fastening not untied this time but broken, and the pot of honey I had placed in it sparkling, as if licked clean by a beast's greedy tongue. This sight confused me, especially since I could not find the slightest sign of any clavo either in the woods or around the tree.

As you might imagine, this discovery made me change all my plans. I rushed that very evening to replace the saquetoun and to fill it with the best food I could find, mostly some dried prunes and grape must preserves my nieces in Arles had sent not long ago by way of a local fisherman. Unfortunately, a low clump of grass right under the juniper kept the ground from being marked by clavo, but I did not dare to uproot it, for fear of scaring off the creature drawn here by hunger. I was, of course, thinking about the one who so confounded me in the marsh, but I wanted to be certain. The sight of the saquetoun emptied like this made me wonder. To tell the truth, despite my qualms, I was consumed by a desire to see the Beast again, and also to hear once more the strange voice that roiled my blood and kindled a fire in my breast.

I arranged everything as best I could. Because I needed to bring my animals to the Grand-Couvin marsh and could not neglect my work just then, it was several days before I could return.

It made no difference to me whether I rode Vibre or Clar-de-Luno now. Ever since the scene I described above, Vibre had remained completely docile. I had no doubt that he was forever tamed. I captured him, let him loose on the manado, and captured him again, without finding the least trace of wildness. Quite the contrary. As I have said, he stood still as soon as he saw me and sometimes even took a few steps to meet me; he let himself be peacefully tethered without making any effort to escape. I often must resort to trickery to capture horses that have borne the saddle for years, but this one, only recently broken in, proved easier to handle and far gentler than Clar-de-Luno.

As soon as my work left me some leisure, I returned to the woods to see how things stood. Again I found the saquetoun empty and the little pot inside the canvas completely clean. Just as before, I could not find the slightest track, no matter how hard I searched. Still, thinking I might succeed in this way, I took pains to sweep and level the sand at the foot of the tree, wherever it was not covered by greenery. But, alas, I discovered that a bull—and a big one at that—had rolled around on the stirred-up ground, as I could see from its body's imprint, along with clavo and fresh dung. Although I searched carefully and got down from my horse to better examine the uneven earth, I found nothing that could satisfy me in the least.

But, understandably, my eagerness was growing. And so, right then and there, I made a new decision and devised a plan I hoped would clear up all my doubts. That day, May 27, the sky was clear, although at first the night was moonless. I dined early on a stew of mullet I had caught at Pouncho dóu Lioun, then took Vibre, whom I had tethered beforehand to one of the posts by the stable. After refilling the saquetoun with nuts and preserves, I tossed it over my shoulder and mounted Vibre bareback, ready to head to that part of the woods where, for so many days now, I have watched for the phantom that haunts me. When I remarked on Vibre's tameness and extreme docility earlier, I forgot to mention that he had not reacted when, a few days before, I mounted him without a saddle, something that especially irritates young horses.

That was what I wanted to do that evening. I will soon explain why.

And so I left, quietly skirting the radèu, careful to muffle Vibre's steps as I tread on the far edge of the wet sand along the margin. My cloak was draped over my mount's neck; in my hand nothing but my gardian's staff; on my shoulder the saquetoun's cord; and in my pocket my knife from Arles—as good for hacking a branch of juniper as for skinning a dead cow or slicing a live wolf's belly, which I had to do in the Aigo-Morto pine forest, just three years ago last January. Of course, so as not to be given away, I had carefully locked my dog Rasclet in the cabin.

After fording Nègo-Biòu Gaso, as dangerous as its name implies, but which I cross daily, I halted at the tip of Radèu-Long, not far from where I wanted to go. I leapt gently to the ground and hobbled Vibre's forelegs. Then I untied the seden, which I had wound *en mourraioun* around his muzzle, the way we do when we ride bareback and want to control our horses without bit or bridle. I was hoping that this way my horse would graze peacefully, without bolting, for as long as need be. I also knew that in this wasteland the sight of a seemingly bare, free horse would not connote human presence, and so no living being, no matter how wild, would be scared off. I could be alone, without making a sound, free to stay where I was as long as I wished. For I had decided to solve what I saw as yet another mystery: I was quite sure I was not dealing with any ordinary animal, but, if it was the Beast, how did it manage to make me not see its steps? On the other hand, if it was a man—which I did not at all think—I wanted proof, and, however ill-starred our meeting might be, I knew that with my staff and my knife I would come out ahead. Which is why, after hanging the saquetoun as I always did and carefully wrapping myself in my burnoose—the night's damp in the lagoons is penetrating—I hid as well as I could in a thicket of mastic, determined not to stir from my blind until I either attained my goal or something unforeseen chased me out.

As I have already noted, the night was cool and clear, but the newly full moon would be rising soon. I stayed a long while, entirely at ease, hearing nothing move around me, but listening to the whistles of distant curlews, the honks of nearby flamingos, the clamor of a thousand frogs. The dim shadow of a low-flying raptor brushed my hideout, then disappeared. Luckily, I had thought to face north, and I felt a brisk, light breeze fanning my face; otherwise, marauding mosquitoes would most likely have forced me to move no matter what. Little by little, all the hidden wildlife that had been startled by my approach began to move about again. In a nearby buckthorn, I heard what sounded like a fairly large animal foraging at length. But I could not see a thing. Soon after, the moon broke through. All at once the woods brightened and the shadows on the ground grew darker. It was then around ten o'clock, and a silent peace was spreading through the night. As for me, I was perfectly still, holding my breath; although my legs were falling asleep, I was careful not to make the slightest sound. A big *béu-l'òli*, hunting, landed on a juniper branch. I could see it as if in full daylight. It stayed awhile, studying the saquetoun with round eyes, and then, as if frightened, it spread its wings with a brief cry and dove into the milky calm air, appearing to swim away. Not long after, a lithe, slithering fox appeared, all silvered by the moon. Glistening, it slipped to the foot of the tree, where it sat on its rump, its nose in the air, sniffing like a dog. But suddenly it darted into the thicket, most likely because it had smelled me.

My legs were growing stiff, and although it cost me, my sole effort was to stay still. I waited a long time before anything else happened. The night hours unreeled, marked only by the murmur of all the sounds made in silence by the creatures of this wide expanse. Around me, the buckthorn, juniper, and mastic twigs never stopped crackling and bristling in little bursts. Yet I heard nothing that might trouble an ear like mine, long accustomed to the sounds of spring nights. As it flowed by, time seemed endless.

But soon I heard something new. It was a muffled, recurring beat, arriving from afar, like the steps of a large beast walking. Now and then, it seemed to stop, but it started right up again. Soon it mingled with the rhythmic splash of mud and water. And then I heard the rustle a heavy beast makes as it thrusts its way through brush. Despite myself, my heart was pounding with impatience and desire. I gripped my staff and clutched my knife, open in readiness in my pocket. Minute by minute, the sound approached, growing louder. Now it was arriving right beside me, and I heard a heavy panting in the night air. The closest buckthorns and mastics parted to reveal a large pair of horns and then a black neck: it was one of my bulls, pausing at the center of the narrow clearing near where I had set up my blind. In the moon's bright light, I easily identified him—it was Bracounié, a male with a frizzy forehead who had just turned five this spring. He sniffed for a long time toward the north, leaned lightly westward, stifled a low, and then set off again at the same pace, peacefully, like an animal who knows where instinct calls him and who does not need to seek his path. A few moments later, I heard him splashing through the gaso.

This sight did not surprise me too much. I had of course tonight, like every other night at dusk, driven the animals back from the Enforo. I suspected that the bull—during this season when cattle grow lovesick—had picked up in the wind the scent of a nearby cow, a solitary beast wandering through Bardouïno or Cacharèu; drawn by the lure of the female, he had parted from the manado. But I had not concluded my thought before I heard the same racket, just where Bracounié had emerged. It only grew louder and louder as another bull pushed its way through no more than a few feet from me. But because it never came out of the thicket and its horns were laid back on its neck as it walked, I could not identify it. I thought that this one too was headed in the same direction, having sniffed through the night the same warm scent.

But when I heard and then saw a third animal following the other two (this time it was Liouno, one of my young cows); when I counted, one after another, as many as nine; when I saw a group of a dozen pass by all together—when I recognized the hurried trampling of a whole manado on the march—I could no longer stand it, and, hiding as best I could, I slowly withdrew from my blind. I counted a total of two hundred seventy-four, all mine as far as I could tell, but since I keep watch over more than three hundred beasts on the Riege, I think, despite the moon's brightness, I might have been mistaken, unless the others had stayed in the woods or taken a different path.

As they waded through the gaso, all the beasts I observed seemed to be following a well-marked trail. They plodded along at a steady, even pace, as they do in the morning when I lead them to drink or when, driven through the marsh, they smell the scent of fresh reeds in the air.

I listened carefully for a while, to be quite sure they had all passed, not wanting, if there were more arriving from behind, to frighten and turn them from their path. But finally hearing nothing more coming, I rushed to the spot where I had left Vibre, and where, although hobbled, he was straining forward and whinnying, eager to follow the manado. Releasing him from his fetters, I hastily wound my cord in mourraioun around his nostrils, mounted him, and began to follow the distant line of bulls I could see crossing the lagoon one after another. I curbed Vibre's steps so the bulls could move freely and so as not to risk their turning aside if they saw me. Yet I was sure they had not sensed my presence, for they were padding against the wind through mud and water.

Bracounié was the one leading them. Everyone knows that wild bulls choose a leader among themselves, or in any case they acknowledge the one who proves the bravest and most brutal in battle. Because I knew that this spring Bracounié had been made king on the manado, I was not at all surprised to see him leading the train. As soon as he had forded the water and come onto dry land, he did not waver: he crossed the sansouiro at a trot, followed by the whole band at the same clip, then plunged into Grand-Palun, the Great Marsh, where the reeds are thick and the water quite deep at this time of year. I knew I would get soaked at least up to my hips if I were to cross it on horseback. But it made no difference to me, and I had no fear of bad fevers, eager as I was to learn where this adventure would lead. To see almost a whole manado, accustomed for so long to a vast, deserted land like the Riege, heading north like this in the middle of the night, without being goaded or provoked: I had never seen anything like it, nor, I warrant, has any other gardian, ever since manados have existed under the dome of the sky. Without worrying about another thing, I wanted to know; anyone in my place would have felt the same. I painstakingly crossed Grand-Palun, getting even wetter than I expected. Because the bottom is especially unstable and treacherous, I kept slipping into mud holes from which, with great thrusts of his back, stumbling and half swimming, Vibre barely extricated me. Through the course of that night I owed my life many times over to this horse. Indeed, the sight of those bulls he longed to pursue spurred that ardent creature on, giving him the strength to handle whatever befell him. Because I wanted to stay close behind my bulls, I did not waste time trying to find the passages I knew that could take me safely through the marsh.

Just as I was reaching solid ground and emerging from the water, the last bull disappeared into a thicket of tamarisks that borders the marsh right there. I paused, as much to let my horse catch its breath as to see at more leisure where the troop was now headed.

I dismounted in the middle of the thicket, spread the branches, and moved forward carefully, eager to know but hesitant, because I could hear a swelling, muffled sound, like the steady roar of rushing, overflowing water. At the same time, I thought I heard a kind of whistling coming toward me.

Thinking, not without reason, that the noise of splashing during my passage through the marsh was still echoing in my deafened ears, I inched forward bravely, unafraid, yet careful to keep Vibre behind me and not to show myself through the branches.

But suddenly my blood ran cold and my whole body turned to stone, as if the earth had opened under my feet and I had heard, from the four corners of the universe, the trumpet blast on Judgment Day.

I, Jaume Roubaud, the Pockmarked, saw these things during the hours of that night. First, pushing aside the tamarisks that hid the sansouiro from me, I saw the immense salt flat and the calm, distant lagoons shimmering as always in the moonlight. But soon after, distraught as I was, I recognized the Beast. Upright and naked, he was standing on what we call an *auturo*, a flat knoll covered with short grass, while all around him, a live black throng wheeled in an endless swirl. Thanks to the moonlight, I could see gleaming backs, wild eyes, shining horns. Nearly all the wild bulls of the Camargue must have been there. And, minute by minute, from all ends of the horizon, I could see new bands approaching. First, from far away, I would see a moving shadow swell as it slid beneath the moon; then all of a sudden a manado would appear, the bulls ceaselessly trotting, muzzles down, heads swaying as they plunged into the circle. I saw my two hundred seventy bulls mingle and vanish, like waters from mountain streams that flow into the Rhône and disappear. And the circle continued to grow, to form a dark, teeming cluster around the Beast, like a swarm of bees that, lured from their hive by spring's thirst, intermingle in love's madness. That was when I realized that the Beast, upright at the center, was mastering the bulls by his own power and whim. I felt his will summoning the bulls from a distance, driving them across marshes and plains, blowing into their blood this frenzy that swept them away. Beneath their wild trampling, the battered sansouiro seemed a huge threshing floor. I saw a few more of these late troops as they arrived. The last appeared from the north and was soon lost amid the others in the whirling throng. I heard nothing but hoofbeats, pants, the clang of clashing horns. The moon was at its highest just then. As they leapt, their backs glistened like waves. Many of the bulls looked as if they had come from far distant manados. As they passed through a moonbeam, I could see the reflection of their wet, steaming hides and recognized those that must have forded deep lagoons or one of the two Rhônes.

Always, and without stop, they whirled. More and more quickly it seemed, from moment to moment, more and more quickly. As he raised his arm—so dry and so black—the Beast, with brisk signals, drove the train. Maddened, they flung forward. With his gestures, as with lashes of a whip, he harried them. The more quickly they whirled, the more the circle seemed to widen and spread around him.

And then I saw him suddenly bring to his lips something I could not clearly make out. Yet I thought I recognized an instrument like the one goatherds use. And from this strange pipe, without changing place or position, he began to draw sounds. I heard, amid the animal babble, a wild, piercing music that wrung my nerves. At the first call, the animals, suddenly gripped, stood still, but they started up again right away, driven more strongly by the mysterious melody. They whirled, adapting their pace to it, now slowing down almost to a walk, now leaping and flying in a wild gallop; and the Beast, like a horseman who, on a well-trained horse, enjoys loosening or tightening the reins, seemed to feel a cruel pleasure as he fanned or tamped down their frenzy.

I saw this abominable sight. I saw it unfold before my eyes for a time I could not rightly measure, but which must have lasted several hours. The Beast played the pipe and his eyes glittered. Little by little the music grew regular, and the horde of bulls now turned at a trot, circling the auturo in an immense wheel. When the Beast, intensifying the rhythm, struck the ground with his hoof, the huge manado set off at a gallop. There were, I am sure of it, at least several thousand wild beasts there. A time came when the galloping no longer ceased. Minute by minute, it grew more and more crazed. At each step, I expected to see the troop of exhausted beasts fall to the ground, entangled.

As for the music, it would be hard to say exactly how it affected me. An overwhelming terror gripped me from head to toe; something burned my throat and belly as it passed. I felt my spirit shiver and my flesh faint, as if my blood had been drained. My legs beneath me quaked. An agonizing sweat soaked my canvas smock. And behind me, I felt Vibre's warm breath as he snorted in fear against my shoulder.

Suddenly, the Beast quit playing, raised an arm, and the horde, stopping short, set off again at the same speed but in the opposite direction. Three times I saw this about-face, and the overpowering music would immediately begin again. Whenever the troops reversed direction, their momentum made the animals shove, fall onto, and trample each other. Terrified, I could not take my eyes from the Beast's face, illumined by the moon and transfigured by a wild joy. A mysterious, cold fire seemed to light up the cheekbones and hollows of the eyes. Whenever it stopped blowing, I saw the dark mouth distend in a grotesque grin.

The Beast began to play again, and each breath made the thin skin on its sides and chest puff out hideously. The faster rhythm made the galloping more breathless. I heard a few harsh, brief bellows emitted by bulls gored by horns or trampled in the melee. Two or three times, I glimpsed the Beast rock on its hairy haunches, arching its back and breast.

It was then that the moon, completing its journey, vanished into the west, as if all at once. I did not move. I clearly saw in the shadows the great animal wheel slowly come to a halt and disperse. I saw the troops reform and, without missing a beat, each take up the path toward its manado. I watched mine reassemble and, with Bracounié at the head, slowly move into the mud of Grand-Palun. Right afterward I looked for the Beast, but it had disappeared.

Which is why, hastily mounting Vibre, soaked and shivering like me, I took off as fast as I could, my soul tormented and my blood fevered. When I reached the cabin I released Vibre and, completely worn out, stretched on my bunk, but not without having first, before falling asleep, used the blade of my knife to score a long gash on my left arm.

The next morning, the scar kept me from thinking I had dreamed. To be even more certain, I mounted my horse and retraced more or less the same path I had taken the night before. I followed my own tracks as far as Radèu-Long, and recognized, as I went by, the dense thicket where I had kept watch beside the tree. I saw my saquetoun, still full, hanging from its branch. I skirted Grand-Palun, went all around it, and observed the beasts' track where it entered the water and again where it emerged. On the gray sansouiro, on the other side, around the auturo, I saw with my own eyes a great ring of trampled earth standing out, solid and dark.

I did not linger long because my fever had returned and I was shivering as I swayed in my saddle, even while the blood in my veins burned my body.

When I went to round up my beasts—which I could not do until very late—I found them scattered on the other side of the woods, near Damisello. As I counted them carefully, I could easily see that this time not one of them was missing. I could not help but notice that their hides were dull and most of their flanks were drooping. Bracounié, standing off to one side, seemed listless and ill, not wanting to eat. As I drew closer, I saw he had been gored in his belly and the flesh was already festering. When I went to round up the others, I left him free to do as he pleased; standing still, he watched us depart.

Although I was consumed by a burning thirst, I also let two whole days go by without tasting any food. But my body's sickness was trifling, and soon over. Rather, it was the terror and anxiety in my soul that poisoned my solitude. Unable to resolve to speak, I felt unbearable shame; but even more cruelly than at first, I was haunted by fear. Since this horrid being had not fled the Riege, was I at risk, at every moment, of meeting it on my path? Having already seen all that I have recorded, I wondered how far my terror could go; lacking the courage to face anything more, I feared for my sanity.

Another fear also weighed on me. I thought I had conquered it earlier, but deep down I sensed it being reborn, stronger than ever. How could I be sure that my guilty silence would not cause me to lose my soul forever?

I had seen, I was sure of it, a Sabbath of the beasts on the sansouiro: I had seen the other—the devil perhaps, the creature with the legs of a goat—fill them with demonic fervor. I confess that, standing in shadow and hidden, alarmed by such a sight, I had again tried the power of prayer and the Christian cross. I have to say it had no effect at the time; but it was not much later that the moon disappeared and everything returned to its natural order. I no longer know what to believe. I do not know.

Despite what I decided at first, should I not tell all? What is the use of deluding myself? The peace I find confessing here is not complete. So much has happened that I could not foresee. Should I not ask the Holy Father Abbot to hear me at the tribunal of Penitence and there, humble and sincere, admit all?

But how to find the courage? How, now that, in addition to the reasons that have held me back since the first day, another has been added that I cannot ignore?

My confession complete, would I not have to prove such astonishing claims? Would they not seek the Beast? I am sure they would hunt it. The Beast? Now that I know its power, I fear it. I believe it will know how to avenge itself. But above all, how can I betray it? I have pity for it. I can already hear the hunters' shouts through the lagoons and radèu, the horsemen's trumpets destroying the great peace of the Riege. I see the hunters, galloping across the sands of Mournés, losing their way in the mirage, while the old carcass, fleeing, black with mud from the lagoons, slips from one bush to another. I see its anguished eyes and weak limbs, trembling and stiff. This must not be. Alone, struggling every day within myself, I see all this only too clearly. All of it: the Beast encircled and captured; the Father Abbot exorcising this demi-demon in the sunlight; and the miserable creature bound, beaten perhaps, dragged behind horses to the Abbey. For what crime, to what torture? I do not consent to this agony. More and more, I dread the reproach of its poor, frightened eyes. Ever since the day when I could not bear its suffering, ever since I helped it, when I saw a man's tears flow down its face in front of me, I carry this friendship in my blood, like an illness—despite the repulsion and horror that, from time to time, I cannot resist. How can I speak?

These are the thoughts that endlessly do battle within me, ever since the night, when, hidden in the tamarisks near the Emperiau baisso, I saw that live wheel whirl. One after another, they overwhelm me. Strange. The farther back in time the events recede, the more power they acquire. Remain silent? Is not anything better than this torment?

But my suffering is nothing; it is anxiety for my soul that weighs on me today. When I began this journal, I claimed that no one should suspect Satanism or sorcery at the heart of this matter. Am I entirely sure of that? Is it not, in any case, my duty to confess to my spiritual master, to whom I owe an accounting of my sins? I go, and I feel I can no longer carry this unbearable weight.

I must deliver my secret. Whatever I do, I do not know what will happen to that creature. But as for me, do I risk nothing? In hearing the account of what I have seen around the Vacarés and on the Riege, they will perhaps take me for a madman or for someone possessed by the devil. All the better, since it would be on me that the torture would fall. The torture? My God! Will they limit themselves to confining me in one of the Abbey's dungeons? I know them, those dungeons; I would die there. Then there is the questioning. People say it is an unbearable ordeal, which, innocent or not, no one can withstand. I am innocent. Sant Jaume, my patron, will sustain me. I pray to him each evening, lifting my head up toward the path of stars that bears his name. I must speak. And if they take me for a sorcerer? A sorcerer? Simply for having seen? Often, they do not need anything else. Who can forget the story of that salt-seller . . . ?

Enough! Whatever they want to do, let them do it to me. I must speak and I will speak. Tonight, soon, when I finish writing, I will prostrate myself in front of the little cross hanging here in my cabin, and which, with this journal, is all my sainted uncle left me on this earth: it is a relic in front of which I would not know how to lie. I will recite my Act of Contrition; I will promise what I know I must. And tomorrow, as soon as I have eaten, as soon as I have visited my animals, I will saddle Vibre and go to the Abbey to make my full and complete confession.

To the Abbey or to Vilo-de-la-Mar? One or the other. Better the Abbey, perhaps.

As for these pages, when I will have delivered their secret to the Father, he himself will judge what is best. If he commands it, I will destroy them.

I will leave tomorrow. Tonight, a great peace settles over me. I am fully resolved. I will speak.

November 12

I did not speak. All summer and part of the fall separate these lines from those that came before. If I take up my tale again, it is because, having returned to the Riege a few days ago, I feel all my torment renewed.

Here we are already at the twelfth of November. It was early June when I left. Having written here what I had to write, as you have seen, I lay down that night. The next morning, I rose as usual at daybreak, having forgotten neither the resolution I had made after so much back and forth, nor the oath I had taken. This thought, quite the contrary, was the first that came to me when I awoke. And, moreover, I was doing my best to strengthen it. Everyone knows only too well how our thoughts sometimes seem to do an about-face after sleep has worked on them. I had sworn: I had no regrets, but I later realized that deep down—without wanting to admit it—I was ready to welcome anything that could honestly postpone keeping my promise. I felt less keenly all the anxieties of the night before.

Still, I was getting ready. I saddled my horse and, although I was not very hungry, I was making my breakfast so as not to leave on an empty stomach for Vilo-de-la-Mar, where I planned to see the priest before going to the Abbey. Suddenly, I heard my horse whinny, as if in response to another Camargue horse. Just then, a horseman's shadow loomed at my cabin door, and I rose from the table to see who it could be. I was stunned to find Bon-Pache, my brother, who started to laugh as he dismounted.

"So, Jaume, how's your appetite?"

My eyes on his, I shook his hand heartily, my other hand resting on his shoulder, *à la gardiano*, for it had been a while since we'd seen each other, and I answered, without really meaning it.

"Yes, yes, thank you, everything's fine—"

"Will you hurry and pack up, my brother, the Father wants us to take the bulls to spend the summer, either in the marsh of Saumòdi or in one of the meadows of Coustiero."

"Listen—"

"There's no 'listen,' as you very well know. When the Father commands, we must obey. He knows more than we do, he knows the animals' needs, and besides, he's master. Come, give me something to eat. All I had this morning was a little garlic soup before leaving the Pinedo, and I'm starving."

I sat my brother down at my table, and like me he had an anchovy and a strong onion seasoned with oil and vinegar, along with a hunk of sheep cheese. Then, as a treat, I opened a jar of plump huckleberries preserved in vinegar and honey. While he relaxed after the meal, I gathered my clothes and whatever else I needed, including my fishing and hunting gear; then I placed it all in two baskets to fill Pavoun's ensàrri. A little later, having watered our horses and cinched their saddles, we set out to scour the woods and drive out the bulls so we could make an inventory of them as we always do before leaving the region for a while.

I cannot express the burning anxiety that, at every instant, choked me. As I went from one bush to another, tracking the bulls as we do at such times, crying "Oi! Hoho! Oi!" and striking branches with my staff, I was gripped by a single, unshakable thought. It was the fear, renewed at every step, that I would suddenly see the thing that I alone knew tumble in front of the horses, the thing that I so feared being glimpsed by other eyes. I was careful to shout as loudly as I could and to create a great tumult that carried far into the radèu. And I encouraged my brother to do the same, secretly hoping to warn the Beast of this strange voice and presence in the woods.

"Shout," I urged, "these animals are hard to dislodge when they're dug in for a long time and their gardian's voice no longer frightens them."

But I could not keep from jumping in my saddle each time an uprooted beast suddenly came bounding out from some mastic or tangled juniper. I must confess, too, that I was leery of my brother, a sly devil who can spot all kinds of things with his gardian's keen eye. I knew I would be in trouble if he wanted to question me about some particular clavo. He asked me nothing. Only, once the manado was rounded up on open ground and we were circling the animals to keep them together and count them easily, he frowned and spoke, not looking at me.

"I really don't understand what's wrong with your animals, but may the devil take me if they're not very lean for the season, what with all the grass still here. And you, for sure, you look as if you've caught some fever—for here you are, all skin and bones, with a face like *Ecce Homo*. The Father's not wrong, then, to give you a change of scene."

He said nothing much more, except, when we were setting out, he remarked, without making much of it, "I say, Jaume, if I were in your shoes, herding on the Riege, I think I'd make it my business to eat some of that good ham. It must be crawling with big boars around here."

I breathed a sigh of relief, knowing full well that, just a few days earlier, he would have found the beasts along the shore, worn with fatigue and their flanks wan, without my being able to explain why. What would have happened then? I was also relieved for another reason, but without admitting it to myself. Because, even while bringing me close to the Abbey, this unexpected leave-taking forced me to put off fulfilling my vow.

That very evening, with no trouble at all, our whole manado entered the vast grazing lands known as Courrejau, where my brother and I left the bulls in the hands of two gardians in charge of *acoussouna*, that is, keeping them together all night in a tight group, while we sought beds in the cabins of Galejoun.

I will not here recount my summer, whose comings and goings have nothing to do with the subject of this narrative. For a gardian, the summer months, from one year to the next, are all alike. Everything went along as usual and according to the customs of bouvino. More than once, by the Father's order, we had to lead our bulls through villages on holidays—to make them run in the squares in chariot rings. We did this at Eimargue, in Queilar, and in Galargue-sus-l'Auturo. Everyone knows to what frenzy these games drive the locals. In the town of Vau-verd, one man lost his life.

Whatever the case, with respect to the strange memories I had carried with me from the Riege, I have to say that, without in any way forgetting them, I felt them lessen with my change of place and, since I was busier and around more people, they ceased to be, as before, an ongoing obsession. As my torment decreased, I began to think I was less bound by a vow that now seemed premature—although I did not renounce the vague intention of fulfilling it later. But seeing that I was now out of danger, no longer entangled in events that plagued me, and with peace coming of its own accord, I no longer felt the need to seek peace. Of course I did not let anyone suspect what I had seen and what had happened to me. I told myself I had suffered a brain fever, due to marsh illness or something else that had driven me to distraction, poisoning me with sorrow and heightening my anxiety. As I rode on horseback with my comrades, I was no longer pursued, except from time to time, by those phantoms, and I hoped that when I returned to the Riege for winter I would be completely delivered.

Here I am, then, back. And, finding myself alone again, I also find my trouble again. For when I revisited the watering holes as my work demands, I could not help studying the surroundings. The Beast has not left. At the tip of Redoun Lagoon, along the strand to the east of Radèu de l'Aubo, and on Radèu-Long, there are clavo. I dread seeing it. Simply the thought of a meeting makes me tremble with terror, but also with keen desire.

I must note that I lost my handsome Bracounié. He died in the marsh of Saumòdi, not more than three weeks after we arrived. He stopped eating and starved, wasting away little by little. When I skinned him for his burial, I saw that the goring he had received had caused an abscess in his belly. This, not to mention my torment and trouble, is what I owe to the Beast. And yet, solely to have glimpsed its clavo, I no longer hear the silence of the desert on the Riege.

I will live now in fear and hope; again I sense roaming around me, always and unendingly, the madness I thought forever banished.

November 18
I saw it. I saw it again.

The weather continued calm and mild enough until recently, but for the past five days the east wind has been blowing up a storm. A howling, icy wind that sweeps heavy clouds into the sky; they will burst as soon as the wind dies down.

I was hurriedly driving the manado back from the Enforo this morning, to lead it into the shelter of the woods, when, just as I was entering the first thickets of Radèu de l'Aubo, Vibre suddenly reared up under me. From the intensity of his reaction, by the trembling that shook his four legs, I realized it must be right nearby. And then I saw it, half-crouched under a buckthorn. It was staring at me with those wild, frightened eyes I had noticed at our first meeting, and it did not seem to recognize me at all. It had grown very thin; in some places its body looked like nothing so much as a hideous corpse. The parched skin seemed stuck to its heavy bones. It was all hunched over, its breast sunken. And on the dark, wrinkled face, nothing could be seen except the hollows of the eyes, where a dying flame flickered. The whole body was crying out with so much hunger and pain that, despite my revulsion, I was drawn in. Its fixed, wild eyes stared at me, then suddenly flamed, crazed, like those of a wounded quarry defenseless in the hunter's hands. The Beast leapt up and abruptly turned its head back, as if preparing to flee. But it only sighed, and I saw its dried-out paw clutch its ghastly breast. It stayed where it was. A thought struck me. I dug through my saquetoun to find some food, but because I had left right after eating, expecting to return as soon as my beasts were rounded up, I had brought nothing with me that day. I was flooded by a great pity.

"Are you hungry? Are you hungry? Tell me."

The Beast did not stir. It simply stared at me with its purely brute look, lost in ignorance and fear. It was as if it had never seen me.

And so, without wavering, I turned my horse and, buffeted by the wind, galloped back to the cabin. The weather was worsening: the gray sea, swelling, was washing over the sands and flooding the lagoons. I dug my spurs into Vibre's flanks. Frantic, I felt a growing madness at this dreadful moment. When I reached the cabin, without bothering to pack them, I grabbed a one-kilo loaf of bread and stuffed my sack pell-mell with nuts and apples. I left right away at the same speed, but as I neared the radèu, I slowed down so as not to frighten the one I was hoping to save. Vain caution. The Beast had disappeared.

I tried hard to uncover it, driving my horse at random through the juniper and mastic; not finding anything there, I returned to where I had first seen it, and, to better follow its track, I dismounted, but I soon lost it in the dense thicket.

I was rushing because the wind gusts were subsiding, threatening to stop from one moment to the next. I was certain the downpour would be violent; without a burnoose, I could not venture far. Yet, without overdoing it, I stubbornly searched the path and scoured the thicket. In this way I combed the width of the radèu and found nothing; still, I decided to hang my saquetoun in the fork of a juniper, in hopes that the Beast's hunger and sense of smell would lead it there.

November 21

It has been raining for three days and three nights.

When the wind suddenly dropped, as it does after great autumn gales, a torrential rain began to fall. It is still now so heavy, I can barely open my door to let in some daylight; although the reed roof is well-pitched and well-thatched, water seeps in everywhere. When I look out through the half-open door, I see neither land nor sky; the falling rain envelops all; above as below, water streams.

The days are endless. Forced to do nothing, I spend them as I can. Despite the darkness, my calèu and the fire's glow allow me to write. I hear nothing but the rumbling roar of the sea, whose breaking waves swell the lagoons. The nights seem long, especially since I never sleep. Now and then I think about my animals, but although this weather might be bad for them, I am not really worried. During the coldest and most lashing rains, there is no better shelter for a manado than the radèu of the Riege. What is more, the animals spent a summer of great plenty. I brought them back in fine fettle; they can withstand worse weather.

Something else is eating away at me. How can I not think, endlessly, about the creature I saw in the woods, looking so ravaged? How gaunt he has grown; he looked so weak and starved. Why is he afraid of me, and where could he be? If he had gone away, I would surely have found his tracks on the strand. But most likely he has not left Radèu de l'Aubo, and now I see him there, or closer perhaps, crouched under a buckthorn, shivering, starving, feeling the ice-cold water stream down his spine.

May the devil take all my fear, all my dread. He is nothing but a poor creature, nothing more. I pity him. Who knows if he will have found the food I left in the saquetoun? If he did not get it right away, the bread must be soaked and swollen from the rain. At the first sign of good weather, I will go out.

November 22

The rain is still falling, dense and cold. The wind is still blowing from the east, and the sea is still roaring, both night and day.

Last night, I had a false alarm. It was already pitch black by eight o'clock. As soon as I had eaten, I went to my bunk, but I could not sleep, because the body never rests when it is not worn out by walking or work. The only thing I could hear was rain splattering the roof and droplets steadily dripping here and there onto the cabin floor.

And then, suddenly, my dog Rasclet rose up, growled softly, and ran barking toward the door. But all at once he stopped and started to howl in a way that made my hair stand on end, from my head to my toes. Then he retreated and crawled under my bunk, where he stayed hidden while he continued to whimper. I rose and, to have some light, I used a *brouqueto* to bring fire from the hearth's coals to my calèu. Although I wanted to remain right where I was, warm and snug under my wool blanket, a troubling thought made me get up. What was disturbing Rasclet was most likely the scent of a wolf or some other wild animal, but I had learned by now what other presence could make him whimper like that. And so, ready for anything, I first crossed myself, then set my lamp down on a corner of the table, took my ficheiroun in both hands, and, despite the water dripping onto the sill, threw the door wide open. I stood there a good while, shivering with anxiety and cold; in a hushed voice, I conjured the evil spirits to depart. But no matter how much I ordered and shoved Rasclet, I could not get him to leave his spot. I did not hold it against him, because he is a brave beast; to act this way, he must have a very good reason, which a human cannot fully understand.

No matter how I tired my eyes searching the shadows, I could make out nothing certain. I must note, though, that twice I thought I saw some dim reflection slip through the rain and the black night. But what can you be sure of, when, all alone at the heart of the Riege, you watch like this in the dark through a cabin's half-open door, fear in your belly and an oil-filled calèu flickering behind you?

November 23

The rain lessened and grew finer during the night. This morning, I could at last go out. Right away, I went to seek my horses; I knew more or less where I would catch them in this weather. Clar-de-Luno was the first one I found, and, glutton that he is, I roped him in with no trouble the minute he smelled some oats. I saddled him and, wrapped in my hooded oilcloth, began to comb through the woods. In this way, I could identify my animals and make sure they had not suffered from the bad weather. All were doing well, including the weakest, a young cow that had calved out of season and was quite lean from having to nurse.

I found my saquetoun, untouched and full, right where I had left it. The bread, heavy and soaked with rain like a sponge, made the sack bulge. I did not open it just then, choosing instead to bring it back to the cabin as is. It will serve to make soup for Rasclet: bread is a sacred food, a gift from Providence, and it is a sin to waste it. But I was overcome by a great sadness. What am I to think from now on about the creature? What has become of him? What is he eating? Aside from a few scant roots and those sweet, fragrant juniper berries foxes snatch when driven by hunger, there is nothing for him to eat at this time of year on the Riege.

Rain, although lighter, is still falling. I cannot go any farther today. Yet it will not be long before the weather changes. Already, there's a stronger chill in the air. But the sea is not calm. I can hear it rolling and breathing as it angrily stirs the distant lagoons. I hardly know why its dull voice fills my heart with fear and unspeakable anxiety.

November 24

As could be expected, the wind sprang up after this long rain. First the clouds fled the west: an unmistakable sign. Now I can see a bright sun flashing over the still stirred-up waters and the shimmering, wet sansouiro. From the north, sharp and brisk, I feel from time to time a point of mistral. If it dries up again, we will have some fine days at the end of November. The weather, as everyone knows, changes with the moon, and today is the first day of the new moon.

The countryside, apart from the woods, is more or less completely drowned; the sea and the Vacarés have swallowed up the low-lying lagoons to create one stretch of water, on which the wooded radèu float like true islands.

I am not worried about winter. My animals, as I have said, came back fat, and the Riege, deserted all summer, has plenty of grass in the thickets. This rain has given us fresh water that will last a long time. No, concern for the livestock is not what troubles me. It is the other I cannot stop thinking about, endlessly. Come what may, I must find him, and if I can help him, I will, no matter what it costs me.

It is too late today. But tomorrow, I will. So that nothing delays me, I will have my horse Rouan sleep here. There is grass and water; the weather today is golden. I can let the animals wander at will from one radèu to the next for a few days.

I constantly see in front of me that huddled body with its drawn face and those eyes dulled by hunger and fear. I think of nothing but that; it is too awful. Whether he is akin to me or not, what difference does it make? I cannot leave him like that.

December 10
Without a break, I search and search. It has been several days already. I rise before dawn, and in a great rush, as soon as I have gulped down my soup, I leave to scour the countryside, now on Vibre, now on Clar-de-Luno.

Alas, the season when nights are long has returned. In the evening, the sun goes down early, and it gets dark all at once. To make matters worse, the weather has grown cold. The mistral no longer blows and it is freezing outside.

Since yesterday, I cannot stop thinking about something that seems striking enough to merit my attention. Along the border of Radèu de l'Aubo, I noticed some clavo—exactly the ones I am looking for. They are fresh, that is certain. Uneven and not too deep, they come to an end in front of a bush at the foot of which the earth has been scratched. I searched all around but found nothing more. That is all. It is not much. It is a sign, though, that counts for something. I should note that wherever the ground is hidden by grasses or branches, the clavo cannot leave a trace, and also where the sansouiro hardens after a frost. I rode around on horseback all day, but it was no use. I did find some other clavo going toward Malagroi, but they looked much older.

Each time I return to my cabin, my heart is weighed down with anguish. But it is not the same as the anguish that poisoned my days and nights before. If I have one regret, it is to have left for so long in need this creature whom I now mysteriously regard as a brother; it is not to have foreseen such suffering.

A great peace spreads over my memories. I think, now, with no fear, about the marvels and mysteries I once believed endangered my soul. I no longer smell the stench of guilty terror and anxiety tainting my most innocent actions.

Now, each evening, I fervently recite my holy prayers. If I have truly observed the wondrous scenes I have recounted, it is because, for unknown reasons, Providence has wanted me to be the witness. I have only one aim now, imposed on me by charity—I truly believe I am bringing aid to one of God's creatures.

December 12
Still, I had to pay some attention to the manado. It is not good for bulls, even in a land as vast and free as the Riege, to wander too much at will without feeling the presence of their gardian. For then they grow wild and too hard to handle.

And so, for several days, I had to abandon my search or, at the very least, to limit it to the area where I now keep my livestock. And so it is that, having taken it up again this morning, I write at this very moment in ferment and fever.

I must note that the east wind, which had died down with the frost, has returned, gusting for the past two days. Who knows if this time it will bring us more rain? We have enough water, more than we need, and I hope, as often happens, to see the wind turn to a tramontane.

Today I went through the western part of the Riege, going by way of the Emperiau baisso. I had not yet noticed a single new clavo there, but to tell the truth, the lowlands have been drowned since the last rain, and, under that surface of water stirred by wind, it is almost impossible to make out a clavo.

In crossing Malagroi at an angle, I passed by Grand-Abime, the Great Abyss, to avoid the quicksand. As everyone knows, Grand-Abime is one of those dreadful pools of ink-black silt, not too wide, but so deep that no rope can reach the bottom. Everything that falls into it is, without fail, swallowed up in the maw of this gulf, as deadly for men as for animals. I had enclosed it with pickets so I could see it from a distance, and those pickets also serve as landmarks to help me find my way. I was careful to plant them where the sansouiro is still firm, a few handspans from the dangerous rim.

I was heading toward Grand-Abime, without at first noticing anything unusual. But as I approached, I saw, right in the middle and all smeared with slimy mud, something that looked like the stump of a dead tree, with what appeared to be two roots at one end. It was on a slant, raised on one side and sunken on the other, already sucked down by the abyss. But because of the distance I had to keep, I could not see it very well.

How long would it stay there in sight, before sinking forever? Not very long, that was certain. This thought suddenly unnerved me. Even as it came to me, I felt—why?—anguish arise spontaneously within me. Why should this dull, filthy scrap matter to me?

I wondered how it could have fallen into the abyss, something, I admit, that confused me at first. But the answer was simple. Carried by the sea's current or by a great wind down some radèu, it had floated as long as the water was deep enough, until by chance it came to rest above the abyss that began to engulf it.

To get a better idea of it, I dismounted and paced four steps from the first stake on the north side. I knew I could not go any farther without myself risking a dreadful death.

And so I undid my seden, wound it in my hand as carefully as if I were roping in a horse or a bull, then threw it, trying as best I could to reach the stump and using the force of my throw to open wide the lasso's loop. But it was no use. The wild wind blowing violently from the sea seemed intent on ruining my best throws, and no matter where I stood, it caught my rope or carried it away, tangling it or tightening the slipknot. On top of all that, my seden was getting muddied and growing heavier each time it struck the pool—so much so that I was worn out with no result, and I left both frozen and in a sweat, my arms aching and my legs soaked. I had eaten nothing since morning.

Because the days are so short at this time of year, I could not resume my quest once I had recovered, but tomorrow, before daybreak, I will go to Grand-Abime, armed with the longest rod I can find, to extend the reach of my rope.

What is there in this wreck, that, deep down, worries and disturbs me? I want to see it up close, I want to pull it completely out of the abyss. By my reckoning, it will float a while longer. In any case, it will be a few days before the mud engulfs it.

January 16, 1418
Here it is, more than a month since I have touched this notebook. I reopen it this evening, although I have very little to write.

The day after the day I wrote about above, I returned to Grand-Abime. I had risen early so I could be there before full daylight. Despite what I had foreseen, the stump had completely vanished. The mud of the abyss is ravenous and works fast. I tried to probe the bottom with my stick, but because I went too far forward, I sank up to my thighs and had great trouble pulling myself out to safety—my blood churning with fear, my body covered with stinking silt.

When I returned, I resumed my search through the Riege. Not a day has gone by without my having carefully searched at least one radèu. I drive my horse through the woods, and with my staff I probe the thickets one by one. I have seen nothing. At the tip of Radèu-Long, I noticed a few clavo, but they did not seem new. My saquetoun, still hanging, remains always full; still, so as not to have any regrets, I visit it regularly and sometimes refill it. I will do this for a while longer; later, I will see. For several leagues around,

I have now searched all the land that emerges from the water at this time of year; as for Redoun Lagoon, it is hardly worth the trouble to go there as it will be under water for at least another three months.

This time, the Beast is dead or gone. I feel that I am alone now, too alone. Barely a year has gone by since, on horseback, panting to capture what I thought would be some fine prey, I rushed, combing through marsh and sansouiro, following the mysterious clavo all the way to the Enforo and along the borders of Badoun. I know that I will carry until my death the poison infused in my veins. A fear, a friendship, a mystery; and remorse, also remorse.

My dog Rasclet is here, lying at my feet; from time to time, he raises his head and sniffs toward the woods, then curls into a ball and shivers in his damp fur. Outside, not too far away, I hear Vibre's heavy steps as, his fore-legs fettered, he leaps awkwardly in place.

Tomorrow I will continue to search. The Beast has left, or else is dead. Otherwise, I will find it. As of now, until I discover something, I think I will no longer write. I will pick up this notebook again only if I have something new to record.

From now on, I want to search, and always to search, without being daunted or drained; despite the fact that too often, for some time now, I think back to that tree stump with its double root, which I glimpsed one evening, sunk halfway in Grand-Abime, and which, the next day, had been completely engulfed during the night.

The Caraco

1

Leaning on his staff, Gounflo-Anguielo was herding cows.

As he gazed out over the vastness of the Camargue, from the stretch of samphire to the dusky pine-covered *radèu* skirting the sea, the dazzling sunlight made his small eyes blink.

It would soon be four o'clock, but the fiery heat had not abated. Above the gray salt flat, a flickering wave came and went, a shimmering breath that widened into pools of distant mirage. On the battered land, salt plants rooted and bloomed in animal tracks. Dryness reigned. Here and there, between clumps of samphire, the scorched ground crackled; in the *roubino*, marsh grasses grew golden like ripe wheat; everywhere, heat had long ago dried up or fouled the fresh water poured into hollows by passing storms.

Nearby, an animal raised its muzzle, brayed softly, then headed seaward. "Oi, Tancredo! Oi!"

Gounflo-Anguielo stirred. He unclasped his hands, stood straight up in his boots to see far off, then swayed like an inchworm for a moment. But everything was in order. The animals were grazing, scattered all the way to the edge of Clamadou; they could stay there for another hour or longer. Calm, he turned back and resumed his place, chin resting on his two fists, staff obliquely planted and casting a shadow like a sundial's needle on the blazing salt flat.

You could say that these bulls, herded now near Queilar for the summer games, were among the lucky ones. Sighing, Gounflo-Anguielo stared at the sterile stretch that surrounded him; in his mind's eye, he suddenly saw green meadows shaded by willows, openwork *bouveau*, ditches brimming with fresh water, lush marsh grass crowned by dozing dragonflies.

Gounflo-Anguielo had been herding bulls for more than thirty years. To see his spare frame and the small neck that bore the scrunched skull above his shoulders, you would never have said he was made for such a life. But no matter! Like all the others, he had the *passioun di bèstio*: he was wild about bulls.

As a child, he'd roamed the Camargue, hiring himself out as a gardian in the manados, choosing to ride the old horses. With his two gold coins a week, he never lacked for something to eat; not counting, as he liked to say, the bad falls and horn blows throughout the year. But he was not much of a talker. He preferred solitude to the company of other gardians. For a long time now, his scrawny mug and red-rimmed eyes had made him the butt of jokes on the manado, and more than once his mustache, short and bristly like mares' manes after their spring clipping, served for an evening's good laugh. And yet, if it weren't for the drought, he would have been happy enough herding his little troop of wild bulls on Grand-Radèu. He eyed them one by one; those in the distance looked no larger than rats. A few feet away, black Tancredo and golden Caramèlo were eating beside Galino, whose white muzzle moved up and down with every mouthful. But saints alive! how worn they were now by thirst, and how, day by day, their skin grew duller and duller.

Suddenly Galino raised her head and a few cows around her also stopped eating. Alarmed by something unseen, a two-year-old stole away to the left at a trot.

Not knowing what was happening, Gounflo-Anguielo whistled softly, trying to calm the animals.

"Huhu! Huhu!"

Her nostrils dilated, Liouno looked fierce as she pawed the ground and snorted.

"Good God, what's wrong?"

A sound echoed softly through the samphire; when he turned his head, he saw a dim shadow graze the water near him.

It was a dark-skinned girl, a Caraco, whose bare feet he had not heard as they padded on the smooth sansouiro; disheveled, she was now stretched out on top of some samphire. Her eyes half-shut, she was silently rubbing her bronzed forehead with the back of her hand. Gounflo-Anguielo studied her. She must be sixteen, at most. Her checked jacket and skirt of coarse, tawny silk brought out her body's youthful, firm curves. Thick brown curls tumbled down her forehead. A Caraco to be sure, like the ones who ride their caravans to the May festival in Les Saintes-Maries-de-la-Mer. Parasites and thieves, you could say, but what was this one doing here in the middle of bull country, so far from the well-traveled roads?

Half up on her knees, she pointed to the roubino and, exhausted, asked him a question.

"Tell me, is there any water to drink in this big ditch?"

He saw she could go no farther. He looked again at her eyelids, her trembling lips, her whole face, its natural darkness further blackened by the sun's rays. He bent down, handed her his flask, and as she greedily gulped, her head thrown back, Gounflo-Anguielo watched life flow back with the wine into the little Caraco's blood.

The sun was already going down. It was time to climb onto his horse and drive the cows in. From a distance, the girl watched the man approach the white Camargue horse, shake a feedbag filled with oats in front of it, then straddle it bareback after having first wound the rough rope around its nose to make a *mourraioun*. He rode back and forth, chasing one animal after another across the plain; little by little, the whole troop gathered, closed ranks, and set off. Through the clamor of bells, you could hear his shouts.

"Oi, Tancredo! Oi, la Loubo! Oi, Caramèlo! Oi!"

The animals trampling the sansouiro raised a fine dust that glowed red in the last gleams of the sunset.

When, one by one, the troop had vanished into the sands, Gounflo-Anguielo found the Caraco waiting for him behind the pines.

"Won't you tell me, little one, how you came to be lost so far away?"

Clearing her throat, she replied. It was simple.

Her father had died a while ago in Coudougnan, the Languedoc village where, as everyone knows, many Caraco live. An aunt who had at first taken her in was sending her to Seloun, to one of her relatives who'd grown rich selling horses at the fair. She had been on her way for two days, but, wandering from copse to copse and path to path through Séuvo-Riau on this side of the Rhône, she'd gone round and round for a long time until, worn out by the sun, she'd finally reached the spot where Gounflo-Anguielo was herding.

He'd stopped to light his pipe; now he drew a few puffs so he could think straight. The quickly spreading darkness was still cloudless. At the close of this summer day, a belated gleam from the sunset flickered in the distance. In unseen rays, heat rose from the earth as from a brick oven.

Gounflo-Anguielo stretched out his arm.

"Do you see, little one, the path that skirts the roubino over there? If you keep it always to your right, without straying, you'll reach the main road. When you come to the Rhône, call out loudly for the ferryman. He'll take you across. On the other side are plenty of farms where you can spend the night."

But she shook her head.

"Your farms don't welcome Caraco for the night. The barking dogs frighten me. I'll sleep somewhere, don't worry. I've spent other such nights when, as a little girl, I followed the caravans."

They took a few steps together before a thought struck Gounflo-Anguielo.

"And where, then, will you eat?"

She shrugged as she answered.

"I'm not hungry. I already ate a piece of bread before you gave me something to drink. And, on top of that, I'm too tired to go any farther."

Another thought remained, hidden. He realized she was going to stretch out in the darkness, all alone, right there in the samphire. He saw again his own days of hunger, the nights like this when he'd slept on the sansouiro, having eaten nothing since morning. The gnawing ache in his belly and the fear of the desert suddenly returned. He recalled: A fox, hunting, yelps by the sea; curlews fly past as their raucous calls echo in the silence; all kinds of creatures circle around, secretly joining forces to drive you mad. In the moonlight, the least mosquito dancing near your eyelids seems to be some giant bird. You're worn out with fatigue, sleep hounds you, but you hold back, afraid to see, glinting through your dream, the horns of the wild bull that, with its thick muffled breath, has sniffed you out in the darkness.

And so, having thought some more, he retraced his steps.

"Listen, little one, you'll come with me to my cabin. We'll have some hot soup and then, safe from fevers, you'll stretch out comfortably on the hay in the stable."

2

As in all the world's deserts, news spreads through the Camargue at blinding speed. It's as if it rushes unhampered across the sansouiro, through the free air, in the dazzling light and echoing sound.

The day after the Caraco arrived, it was known at Mas dóu Juge that a woman had crossed the cabin's threshold. By evening, the shepherds of Pin-Fourca would be speaking of it at the Jasso. The next day, it was breathed so loudly in "li Santo" that the postman took a long detour to pass by the gardian among his animals.

"Greetings!"

"Greetings!"

"What's this I hear, Gounflo-Anguielo, that you now have company in your cabin?"

But Gounflo-Anguielo, blinking, stared at him and did not answer.

Soon it had been four days that the girl was here. There was no thought of her leaving.

In the morning, before dawn, when he rose to go to the animals, the man found his bowls nice and ready, the bottle of brandy on the table, the coffee dripping through the big, boiling-hot filter. When he returned at dusk, the soup steamed in the bowls, and the clay pitcher, full of fresh water, swung in the open air. The cabin had been swept, clean linen was drying by the door, and it seemed to Gounflo-Anguielo that it had always been this way. Only, as of the second day, when she was getting ready to go to the stable, he'd calmly taken down his burnoose.

"It's much too hot for me in this cabin. I think I'll sleep better in the hay. You, little one, will sleep here."

And he gave his bunk to the Caraco.

Today, he got it into his head to do some errands in the Saints.

Once the cows were settled far from the borders, he saddled his horse, placed the folded wool blanket under the pommel, and tightened the knots at the end of the straps we use *senso bloucage*. He was rushing because, in all this heat, the biting flies clustered around the bulls seemed hungrier for horse's blood. He wrapped the seden, then bridled the horse quick-quick and fixed the curb; once in the saddle, he called out.

"Hey, little one, what do you want me to bring you from the Saints?"

The girl showed her face on the doorstep—eyes teasing, skin shining, charming brow covered in curls. He gazed at her like this for a moment, then turned calmly toward the Rhône. When he looked back, he saw her smiling and waving.

The heat was still beating down when Gounflo-Anguielo reached the main street at a gardian's pace. The horse's unshod hooves clip-clopped on the smooth cobblestones with dull, brisk strokes. Long used to wide open spaces, the animal shied as it skirted shadows and the houses' dazzling, sun-bleached walls; but the man, ignoring the horse's snorts, dismounted and hitched it in front of the forge.

First, he needed to buy some groceries at Casimer's shop—some ground pepper and coffee, a kilo box of sugar, a big dried cod splayed out like a kite.

He carefully filled the *saquetoun* he always carried over his shoulder, fastening it with its bone buttons. Then, raising his head, he noticed a cluster of little clogs all tied together. It struck him that he might bring a pair to the cabin. Without hesitating, he chose, making his coins ring on the counter as the shopkeeper brought them down with his forked cane.

"Someone asked me to get them . . ."

As he left the shop, he was very pleased indeed. In the west, the sun was lower in the sky above the Rhône. A few men, their siesta over, trailed along the sea.

"O, Gounflo-Anguielo! How are your animals, are they eating?"

"As much as they can."

"We don't often see you in town!"

"But tell me," said another, who'd been eyeing the new clogs, "is it true then that you're hiding a female in your cabin at Grand-Radèu?"

He acted as if he hadn't heard, mumbled "later," and kept going. He felt as if a heavy weight had suddenly fallen onto his back and shoulders.

The horse, well-hitched, was calm for now. Turning down the street to the left, Gounflo-Anguielo entered the butcher shop.

"Hello all. I'd like two mutton chops."

The butcher-woman, who'd been dozing, lifted her head; flies buzzed in the stench of the hazy meat stall.

"Aren't you afraid of the sun, you gardians?"

Still half-asleep, she came back to life, briskly handling the mutton under its red gauze. "Look at these flies, what filth! And your cows, are they doing well? How we need a good rain for the grass . . . Speaking of which," she added with a smirk, "I hear you'll soon be sharing wedding favors with us."

Enraged, he snarled back.

"I hear that in Bèu Ciar, there's a fortune-teller who can make asses talk."

He paid for his meat, letting the door slam as he went out.

He returned to his horse. A stubborn thought was taking shape in his head, driving him. Quick, quick, right now, to return to the open space and free air! If he'd dared, he would have left at a gallop, right there in the street, in the middle of the village. On his way back this time, he wouldn't take the ferry again; instead, a customs officer would bring him across the Rhône at the mouth of the Grau d'Ourgoun.

As he went down the beach road, he was stopped again by some fishermen.

"O, Gounflo-Anguielo!"

"Greetings, greetings!"

With a strong kick, he spurred his horse.

The Narbounés wind that had risen from the sea blew against his tense brow. Its coolness did him good. He felt the gentle wind ruffling his neck, fanning his chest and shoulders, flowing under the thick velvet of his pants and along his scrawny little legs. It came to him like a wave that, as it calmed his whole body, cooled the fire in his blood.

When, more composed, he reached the Grau d'Ourgoun, he filled his pipe. In the shimmering air, you could see the pointed sails of slow-moving little fishing boats; at this hour, the beach boats would not be long in setting forth. Nearby, a pod of porpoises leapt and played in the dazzling water of the estuary.

Standing straight, shielding himself from the wind with his hand, he called out across the Rhône.

"Houhou!"

On the other shore stood the customs house, heavy and square, ringed by a hedge of tamarisk and poplar.

"Houhou!"

A man in shirtsleeves appeared. Gounflo-Anguielo easily recognized him despite the shadow from the kepi perched over his ear. How many times had he not, as a boy, ranged through the farms with Ferren, just the two of them; and later, as a young man, when the horns of the *anoubloun* had torn their pants in the *ferrado*? To see him coming in his boat, cutting slantwise across the current, finally laid his trouble to rest.

When the saddle had been placed in the boat, they pulled the horse through the water. Glistening in the sun like a water beast, the horse walked at the end of the seden, at times submerged from his heaving back to his neck, breathing heavily, snorting two jets of spray. In the stern, you could hear each blow of his snorting nostrils. The gardian chatted about his cattle, the games, the drought ravaging the land. But when they reached shore, the customs officer stopped him.

"You'll come have a drink with me," Ferren said. "It would be strange for Gounflo-Anguielo to pass by Grau d'Ourgoun without clinking glasses with me."

But the other man defended himself.

"No, no, believe me, I don't have time."

He quickly strapped the saddle onto the drenched horse, moving branches from the crupper as fresh water dripped down the mane.

"A drop of absinthe with a little syrup, there's nothing better to quench your thirst and drive out fever."

"No, no, really, thank you all the same. Another time."

He grabbed the mane, set his sole in the big iron stirrup. He was already making tracks when he heard Ferren's voice ring out behind him, bitter and biting.

"O, Gounflo-Anguielo! If I can give you some advice, it's to be wary of Caracos!"

He'd never in his life raised his hand against anyone, no matter what happened; but now he wanted to get down, charge the customs officer, smash his ugly red jowls and bulging eyes with his fists.

A fog that darkened everything now spread around him. He no longer found comfort in the clear sky, the smoke from his pipe, the coolness of night as it fell by the sea.

Without answering Ferren, he continued on his path. Now he was skirting the bare beach scattered with dunes and blue thistles. Because his saquetoun hurt a little, he stuck his finger under the thin cord as he walked; he felt as if the weight of the clogs, suddenly such a heavy burden on his stiffening neck, would drag him backward off the horse and onto the sand.

3

Ever since his return from the Saints, Gounflo-Anguielo had not said a word.

As he came and went, he did his usual work with wrinkled brows and tight lips under his little mustache. Already not much of a talker, he came to meals, filled his plate, and ate.

But that day, the girl, who could no longer stand it, spoke as she served the soup.

"Eat your portion while it's hot, it will unseal your lips."

He turned to her with such a look that she stopped laughing and, surprised, questioned him.

"What's wrong with you now, that you don't want to say a word?"

His fist banging the table rattled the glasses.

"What's wrong is that plenty of people would be better off holding their tongues, because there are some real swine out there, goddammit!"

The curse, blazing from his mouth after so much silence, made him feel better at last.

He soon seemed to think of other things, and, gazing high up into the distance, he went on in a gentler voice.

"Have you ever been to the Saints, little one?"

No, she'd never been, but during the May festival her aunt had bought her a little medallion she always wore. Showing a little bit of brown skin, she slipped her fingers between two buttons and drew out the treasure. It had been so long since she'd wanted to make the pilgrimage. Everyone said it was so beautiful, the descent of the reliquaries by candlelight, the procession of the Boat to the beach where Sant-Bras every year renews the sea's miracle.

Listening, saying yes with little nods, he relaxed fully. When he took his staff to go to his animals, she heard him whistling.

After finishing his siesta under the pines, he looked to see if the cattle were done eating. A few still rested, motionless on the sansouiro, but most had gone toward the woods; all around, you could see calves asleep after suckling.

With a sigh, he got off his elbows, drew himself up, turned around.

Something bright shone in the distance; it seemed to be coming toward him. Little by little it grew, gliding across the sansouiro, white and fluttering like a sail. Some horseman, most likely, some gardian tracking a lost animal, coming to inquire at the cabins of Grand-Radèu. What with the games at this time of year, there was no shortage of escaped bulls.

Kneeling, Gounflo-Anguielo shaded his eyes with his right hand. Yes, it was indeed a gardian. Looking as carefully as he could, he tried to identify him. He saw the erect torso, the slim, lithe profile, and the dangling arm clutching the haft of the long trident.

The lively horse was going along briskly, snorting and tossing its mane in the sun.

Who could it be? No one, to tell the truth, cut a better figure than Master Reinaud.

And so, to be entirely sure, he went forward.

"Look at you, so wide-eyed," said the baile to Gounflo-Anguielo. "It's simple enough. We've just leased the Mejano marsh in Queilar, and, since all the animals here are dying of thirst, we'll lead them this very night to our new pasture. Come, your time off is over. We'll take the young calves by moonlight while it's cool out, and, if we're lucky, we should be passing quietly through the vineyards of Mas de Bourry before daybreak."

A moment later, Gounflo-Anguielo was rounding up his animals. The heat was even more stifling than the day before; since afternoon, dark clouds had been gathering in the west. With all of Reinaud's words buzzing in his head, he straddled his horse bareback and, from one clearing to the next, he chased the trailing animals, beating the bushes with his staff as he shouted the cows' names at the top of his lungs.

"Oi, Liouno! Oi, Caieto! Oi!"

Making his mouth explode, he frightened the little black calves who raced along behind their mothers with their tails down.

In the open, he had to identify the livestock. He counted them on his fingers, losing track in the melee of black backs and tossing horns, amid which the cows were circling in place with their calves.

"Forty-one, forty-two, forty-three . . ."

It was as if he were spellbound, distracted, mixing up the numbers, and he had to start over three times.

Now, heartier, Gounflo-Anguielo was heading back to Grand-Radèu.

The sun was still shining brightly, but the weather was milder. The clouds that gathered at dusk when he was leaving burst in the middle of the night. As he rode along at his gardian's pace, he recalled the hard journey. Because the moon had been hidden by the storm, the darkness had grown even thicker after each flash of lightning. They'd tried to find their way in the sudden light, guided by glimpses of the sansouiro under the blazing sky, of the herd fleeing under the downpour. It wasn't much, two horsemen herding a convoy of cattle in such weather. Reinaud had guarded the front most of the time, while Gounflo-Anguielo, keeping along the sides as much as he could, had ridden through ditches and over ground suddenly swamped by water where the animals splashed. Between two claps of thunder, his voice had risen above the clamor of bells and bellows.

"Ha, ha! . . . Oi! . . . Ha, ha!"

The water, streaming from the concave leather saddle, had dripped down his legs and into his shoes. He didn't care. If only the dry earth would soak up the water like his burnoose. And he'd gone off shouting, moving down the side through the darkness, leaping over levees in one bound, his horse landing on four feet in puddles of wet mud.

At daybreak, in the sad east, more shreds of clouds trailed, but the dawn's white light signaled the end of bad weather.

One by one, Master Reinaud had counted the animals; none had been lost in the storm's frenzy, and, smiling, he'd leaned over in his stirrups.

"Tell me, my friend, who would believe that on such a night our two horses didn't get any cramps? Come, let's go now, and if your pocket's not too soaked, hand me some tobacco so I can roll a cigarette."

As he returned to Grand-Radèu, Gounflo-Anguielo was recalling all this. The rain had washed the grayness from the samphire, and on the mud— where, step after step, each print left a track—the salt was no longer white.

After he'd groomed his horse the night before, the baile had spoken.

"Now that you're rested, you can strap on your saddle tomorrow morning and return to the cabins. Last night's storm must have poured rain everywhere. You'll have to check the watering holes and fix the fences along the way. As soon as I can, I'll bring you a herd of fighting bulls."

He'd left, musing happily about the Caraco.

The Caraco? He thought suddenly about the fishermen in the Saints, the butcher, the fat customs officer Ferren. He took his pipe from his mouth and spat violently onto the ground beside the horse. The Caraco? She alone was worth the whole lot of them. Now, feeling strong as he sat up straight in his saddle, he no longer understood why their words had so wounded him the other day, so much so that he'd returned beaten down along the dunes of Sóuvage.

The girl, he was sure, would have kept in mind what he'd told her as he rushed to leave. What's more, she had the key to his cupboard with enough food for a week, and the jar was full of fresh water.

His hat brim falling a little over his eyes, he couldn't help laughing. How surprised she'd be to see him back so soon!

Oh, how fine it was to return to a cabin that wasn't empty, to sit down upon arrival in front of clean glasses, the wine in the bottle and the table set.

For a while now, he could see the cabins. They were outlined, neat and small, in the clean air: first the biggest, where he lived, with its peak and roughcast walls whitened with fresh lime; then the stable, whose rafters held up a reed roof; and behind them, lastly, the smallest, where the oats and wine were stored, with its rounded rump facing north, low and bulging, looking from afar like a poacher's hut.

Slowly, he made his way. The horse, as he sensed the approach of his manger, sniffed toward the lagoons, whinnied, pulled on his bit.

Gounflo-Anguielo had again started to smile. A few more steps and, once he crossed the roubino, he'd see at the first turn the brown face framed in the shadow of the open door.

But the door did not open; his call went unanswered.

The girl most likely had gone out, since the key was here beside the threshold, under the big stone. Where the devil could she have gone?

While he tied up his horse, he was thinking, looking distractedly all around. Perhaps, when she saw him coming, she'd hidden in the pantry to tease him?

But there too, everything was in order—the red peppers hanging in a row, the dry cod and sausages neatly under glass and safe from rats. As he rummaged around, he banged into the big boots hanging among the bridles and saddles. On his knees, to see better, he half-opened the oat bin. Nothing. So, alone in the stillness, he felt himself grow more and more anxious. Although his knees were stiff from the journey, he climbed the ladder set beside the door so he could watch over the animals. On the highest rung, he stood up straight, took a deep breath, and called out.

"Houhou!"

As far as his eyes could reach, he could see nothing except the samphire's waving, the radèu's dark pines, the sea's calm blue stretching to where the sky came down to meet it. Nothing alive, not anywhere, nothing but a scattered flock of gulls fishing in the lagoons.

Troubled, he went back into the kitchen. He let his eyes range from one corner to the next. The reddish earthenware was stacked up on the scrubbed shelves; the dirt floor had been swept; the tin-plated filter shone in the darkness.

But above the table, a strange slip of paper, some sort of sign, finally caught his eye. It was a sack from the grocer's, stuck to the wall by its corner, covered from end to end with thick charcoal letters. His hands pressed flat on the wood, an anxious trembling in his legs, Gounflo-Anguielo painstakingly read, deciphering word by word the wild writing of these lines that seemed to melt into one another, fluttering like phantoms before his eyes.

"I'm going. Leaving. Thank you."

Little by little, he understood. The Caraco had left.

But why? Where to? He didn't even wonder. From now on, he would no longer see her.

A poison dulled his brain, made his blood boil.

"Gounflo-Anguielo, now you're all alone!"

He'd spoken out loud, the way folks do when they're feverish. And then he'd stood there, dumbstruck, his two fists jammed into his pockets.

Without quite realizing what he was doing, he somehow left the cabin. Calm, he walked slowly along the roubino, dragging his feet. Then he suddenly saw the heels of the two clogs sticking up out of the mud—the clogs the girl had most likely left behind on the grass before going away. Their thick leather vamps shone in the light, gleaming as if still new. But the man's mind was elsewhere. When he spied the clogs, he thought back to his return from the Saints, the fog that had risen on the beach, the too-heavy canvas sack he'd carried on his neck at the Grau of the Rhône. He felt a surge of rage.

He bent down, grabbed the clogs by their soles, and, raising his arm, furiously flung them into the roubino.

Just then, one after another, the frogs jumped, causing the reeds to shiver. One splash was so strong it reached the gardian, who felt the cool spray on his lips.

One of the clogs had sunk into the mud right away and could no longer be seen. The other floated upside down, like a lost ship dancing with each wave.

Evening came.

Now, through the deserted countryside, no animal cry, no tinkling bell. Only the faint buzz of mosquitoes, spawned by the thousands in the new rain.

A great heron, its legs outstretched, tossed its melancholy cry upward.

"Mouah!"

And Gounflo-Anguielo, his head in his hands, collapsed onto the levee; long after the moon had risen over the Pinedo, he still had not moved.

Pèire Guilhem's Remorse

1

Through the large opening that lets light into the animal pens in the arena at Arles, Pèire Guilhem was leaning over to watch his bull emerge. The animal rushed out of the darkness, bounded across the open space between the fences, and then, blinking and ready to charge, it turned to face the first picador.

In the packed stands, hands clapped.

"What did you feed this one?" an on-duty carpenter, his elbows on the fence, yelled from below.

"Hey, Blanquet," the gardian replied, "I swear he ate what the others ate, but bulls are just like men, there's always some good mixed in with the bad."

"They're the same," Blanquet agreed.

A big gray wreck of a horse had just collapsed onto the sand, and attendants in dusty red vests quickly ran in, removed the harness with their staffs, and carried off the stunned picador by his armpits—while he spat up his teeth.

"Hey, toro!"

At the matador's hoarse yell, the bull that had been running along the fence turned, stretched its neck, then lunged at the cape fluttering under its nose. Like a dying flame, the cape seemed suddenly to vanish before its eyes.

The applause mounted.

The carpenter, his blue shirtsleeves rolled up to his elbows, clapped and cried out.

"Now there's a bull, my man! There's a bull!"

Then, without even looking up, he took a few steps back to get closer to the gardian.

"Say, Guilhem, doesn't it hurt you to see such a creature die?"

Pèire Guilhem looked at him and shrugged.

Hurt? Of course it hurt. To tell the truth, he didn't much like these Spanish bullfights. It was a pity, after all, to think about the long years it took to make a strong bull, to see it sacrificed in the blink of an eye by this pack of curs. Oh, well, if he were master . . .

But Blanquet was no longer listening. He was haranguing the men of the quadrille, heckling a picador who happened to be standing not far from the fence.

"Hey Duro! Too bad your lance isn't a little longer, eh? You good-for-nothing! Are you afraid to get too close to a bull like this one? Oh! The swine!"

Out of the blue, the bull had just charged, and the defenseless horse, gored in the neck, backed off, blood spurting from its breast and spilling onto the sand in a thin stream. It took a few steps, trembled in place, then collapsed. Women, shrieking, turned away. Hisses and howls broke out everywhere, chiding the clumsy man.

"*Otro caballo!* Another horse, another horse!" cried the picador, entangled in his stirrups.

But the matador spread wide his cape and again the crowd roared. Tossing aside their long lances, attendants ran through the hubbub to sprinkle the ground with sawdust.

Blanquet, even more annoyed, whistled.

"Did you see that Duro? Did you see him? What did he think he was facing, that rag of a picador?"

He drew himself up, and, turning to Guilhem, nodded toward the horse door.

"Hey Guilhem, take a look at that horse. Wouldn't you say it's a Camargue?"

Pèire Guilhem yawned, turned down his hat brim, glanced coolly at the horseman straddling the white nag in front of the just-closed double door.

Yes, it could well be a Camargue.

What with the saddle and heavy caparison, you couldn't see much of the old horse draped in the arena's trappings, nothing except the neck and head, a thin, bony croup, and four hairy legs that seemed to stagger under the man's weight.

"Poor old nag!" said the carpenter.

Duro viciously spurred the horse and tossed his hat, swaggering.

There were yells and a few hisses.

The attendant holding the bridle ran to the rear, raised his staff, and smacked the horse with a blow that echoed in the half-silence.

"Hey, toro!"

The bull had just charged.

But this time Duro, gripping his long lance near the tip and leaning out of the saddle, thrust with all his weight into the bull's withers. For an instant, you could see nothing but the man's back and braid, along with the beast's loins as he wrenched away. Then suddenly, under the pressure, the horse rose up slightly, shook, staggered, and toppled stiffly onto the sand.

The bull charged and butted the horse again with its head.

It was growing angry.

A horn snagged near the horse's shoulder, slipped under the leather and canvas, and ripped the caparison. Duro was pressed flat the length of the downed horse as the bull began to sniff his legs.

Quickly, a cape was spread; the matador stepped in. A veil masked the beast's eyes, hid the grounded man. And the bull, led astray again, rushed to the other side of the ring, following this foe who made his way in a taunting swirl of cloth.

The crowd went wild. The ovation, suspended for a moment, burst out. Caps and hats and canes rained onto the ring. Amid the uproar, music began to play.

To everyone's amazement, the horse was back on its feet, racing along the fence. As it flew by, an attendant caught it, led it back. And the cheering swelled when Duro, upright in the high saddle, reclaimed his lance and signaled he would return to the fray.

Just then, loud hisses stopped him. People were protesting, on account of the caparison. You couldn't pic on a bare horse like that, you had to change mounts. Pretending not to understand, Duro looked with astonishment at the noisy stands. A banderillero took the bridle and with one stroke turned the nag toward the horse door.

Behind the fence, Blanquet was no longer clapping. His two palms ached.

What a man, that Duro, when he wanted to be!

He blew into his burning hand, reached into his pocket for a pair of cigars, threw them into the ring as far as he could. A great pic, a great pic!

"Hey Guilhem, a great pic!"

But, wide-eyed, he stopped.

Suddenly leaning forward and straightening his long legs, Guilhem had just jumped off the little ladder to land beside the carpenter.

"What's happening to you? Where are you going like that with your trident?" the stunned Blanquet asked.

The gardian was silent.

Standing on tiptoe, he seeming to be eying something on the other side of the ring. With his sleeve, he wiped the beads of sweat off his white face.

"After all," cried Blanquet, "I think I'm speaking to you, and unless you've grown deaf or don't understand me . . ."

But Guilhem elbowed his way forward, shoving the other man aside.

"Goddammit, let me by, it's Pavoun!"

He rushed along the fences, continued down the corridor. A sentry hailed him.

"Hey gardian, what's going on?"

"Nothing, nothing at all."

A banderillero, caught just then by the bull, was shoved roughly in the ring and thrown to the ground. Shouts exploded everywhere. But Guilhem barely turned his head, did not change his pace.

In one burst he ran to the horse door. In front of the stalls, under the stone archway, a thin mare, chased by some attendants, was trotting forward. On the other side, in the darkness, he glimpsed the white tail of a nag, standing still, and a picador, leaning on the saddle bow, dismounting. It was Duro.

Gripping the trident with both hands, Guilhem silently fell onto the picador, bashing him behind the shoulder.

The blow was softened by the sequins on Duro's jacket, but the shock was so strong that, swaying in his saddle, he rolled sideways. As he fell, attendants caught him.

Weighed down by the metal and cloth that protected him in his leather pants, the picador was kicking and flailing; choked with rage, still tangled in his stirrups, he began to hurl insults and curses.

Guilhem's shouts drowned him out.

"Let me go! Let me go, goddammit! Let me go! This horse will not go back into the ring. I'm telling you, it's Pavoun. I know him. An animal like this? . . . A gardian's horse that knows more about bulls than a man does? . . . To make him die by the horn? You band of bastards!"

He was fighting with all his might, throwing punches to right and left at the fools restraining him.

"Here's the owner, he'll take care of it," said one of the lackeys.

Indeed, a big man who'd emerged unexpectedly from the stalls was peering under Guilhem's nose, which he didn't immediately recognize in the dark. Astonished, he took a step back.

"You? You, Guilhem? A steady boy like you? To come and make a scene in my arena? Who could have predicted this? A gardian of bulls, to boot! . . . Will we have to tie you up maybe? But, first, the rest of you, let him go."

Enraged, he thrust his hand into his pocket and drew out his handkerchief to mop his brow.

"So, is it that you've been drinking?"

Sullen, Guilhem shook his head no.

Duro, seeing his enemy freed, leapt to the side with his fists up. But Ricard abruptly stopped him.

"You'll do me the favor of going where your work calls you. You'll explain yourselves, the two of you, after the bullfight. Your place is not here."

Grumbling, the picador turned his back on them, straddled a fresh horse, and settled into the saddle. To tell the truth, he didn't understand much, but the director ordered him, and he had to obey.

"And yet Señor impresario . . ."

The picador gathered up the reins and, unable to hold back any longer, his cheeks suddenly reddening, he poured out his rage in a flood of Spanish words.

Just then, a great uproar arose outside, and he stormed into the corridor. Yells mingled with claps and howls. Whistles rang from the high stands. Out of breath, a banderillero with his cape on his arm stopped under the archway and harangued the horseman.

"Hey, Duro, what are you doing here? Don't you hear them shouting outside? The bull isn't fat, my friend, but you didn't stick it very deeply. Hurry! Cigarron has just fallen in the ring and the public is clamoring for more horses. Your matador, I'm warning you, isn't laughing: 'Go quickly,' he told me, 'find Duro, and if he's asleep in the stalls, I'll teach him a lesson that will wake him up.'"

"It's this damn peasant," cried Duro, spluttering, "this swine of an Arlesian cowherd, may the devil take the bitch that suckled him!"

And swept up again by his anger, he pounded his chest, glaring at Guilhem, invoking all the saints of Spain.

"I've been at this work for a dozen years; I was a picador in Portugal, and last winter in Mexico. But, goddammit! This is the first time I've seen an honest family man mocked in the arena—a man who risks his life to win bread for his little ones!"

He spurred his horse and drew away with the attendants, bending under the low arch as the nag awkwardly jerked forward.

A roar of acclaim greeted his return.

2

Pèire Guilhem shrugged. At this point, none of that mattered. Insults? He didn't even understand them.

Worn out by the battle, the old horse had taken refuge in the darkness at the end of the corridor. Guilhem brought it back gently, carefully feeling out with his sole the rough, black ground where the horse flinched at almost every step.

"Hey there . . . easy! Hey there!"

He led him by the bit, his hand up, whistling to reassure him.

"Don't be afraid, Pavoun, don't be afraid. They won't catch you this time."

Through the archway open to the hum of the arena, the section of fence and stands shining in full sun seemed to make the corridor's darkness even darker. Searching for a brighter spot, Guilhem stopped, started to leave, hesitated, took a few more steps, then spoke to the horse.

"Stay here if you like, Pavoun!"

Pavoun! He looked at him. Those jaws and that unkempt, filthy forehead, with those dull, teary eyes and dribbling muzzle that quivered with old age . . . And yet this was Pavoun. It was still him.

He let out a long sigh, nodded, and then, his mind made up, he shook his head.

"It's okay, calm down, I tell you they won't have you."

The caparison, ripped by the bull's horn, was trailing down the horse's chest like an apron. Guilhem's eyes moved along the horse's legs, down to his fetlocks.

"Damn!"

Suddenly watchful, bending over to see more clearly, he gently touched the wet skin. He wasn't mistaken. It was blood.

"Blood? They would have killed him!"

He straightened up and tossed off his jacket. All his former rage returned. His lips tight, he circled the horse, reaching under the stirrups and straps, feeling the metal buckles with thick, trembling fingers.

That people were allowed to weigh down an animal like this!

Pushed backward, the heavy saddle rolled off in a clang of metal and lay upside down on the ground, its four corners in the air.

He tried to reach under the caparison, to thrust his hand into the wound. He was suddenly repulsed. The animal must be deeply gored. His hand would likely touch the horse's insides, grab a warm pile of guts. Disgusting! He spat.

He stood there, up against the animal's flank, almost glued to him.

And then what? Attacking everyone like a drunkard, getting as worked up in a corner of the arena as on the street, to find Pavoun now bleeding like a pig under his harness, losing his guts? It couldn't be, after all, and so— quick, quick!—he had to see for himself.

Raging, rushing, he moaned again, blew on his fingernails, pulled the leather with his teeth. When the caparison had fallen, he roughly kicked it away, casting aside these elaborate trappings.

And so, trembling with emotion, he bent down, rose up, bent down again. Nothing.

Grasping a fistful of mane, he pushed the thick hair aside with his fingers and uncovered the thin thighs, gently feeling the shanks and belly.

It was hard to believe. Truly, there was nothing wrong with the horse.

The tip of the shoulder and nothing more had been touched. The horn, gliding under the leather, had pierced him lengthwise, just below the skin. A thin thread of little dark drops of blood was flowing down the leg between the tendons and along the valley of the muscles.

Pèire Guilhem rolled up his sleeves.

All his strength returned. He left, rushed toward the stalls, returned with a big pail, and began right then and there to briskly wash the wound, splashing fresh water onto the skin.

The horse shook a little.

"Come, Pavoun, it's all right, you'll see the cabins again. Oh! You might not even recognize the bulls."

He started to laugh.

A loud trumpet blast cut him short, coming from the arena amid whistles and shouts. It was the call for the banderillas.

From the other side of the corridor, the surviving horses, led by attendants, were coming back. When he turned, Guilhem saw the thin mare, surely wounded under its blanket, passing by in the faint light, its four legs stiff, its neck outstretched.

But the suffering of others did not move him.

He still had some luck, this old Pavoun!

He tapped the horse's sunken ribs; the sound echoed.

Standing on the muddy ground, he pressed the wound with his fingers, wrung his big handkerchief soaked with reddish water in the pail.

He was happy.

An ovation rose again, spread, faded under the archway like a gust of wind.

But Guilhem, raising his thumb, turned his back to the arena.

"Listen to them shout, what savages!"

To think that all those people could applaud when the bull rolled Pavoun in the dust—he hated them all equally.

He cleaned the hair that sweat was bunching into little locks along the flanks, tried to untangle the thick tail, used his crooked fingers to comb the mane, all stuck together like a donkey's.

He washed the swollen eyes, sponged the hairy muzzle caked with dirt and snot.

"Go on, that's it, groom him well. By dint of working, you might end up turning him into a handsome fellow."

He was so absorbed, he hadn't heard anyone coming. When he recognized Ricard's voice, he felt a rush of blood pound in his temples, but he did not turn.

Ricard walked all around, then stood to face him, his arms folded across his chest.

"Listen, Guilhem, it's best that I tell you. What you did here today—well, I would never have thought it possible coming from a man like you. No, let me speak. It's just the two of us, isn't it? It's not worth getting angry. But that a gardian should leave his post right in the middle of a bullfight to come and attack a picador, to go at him like a dog in the manger, do you find that right, do you? Do you find that right? And what could he have done, Duro? As long as he pics when the time comes and mounts whatever horse he's given, nothing can be said against him. He's paid to do just that, as you well know. And so, what did you have against him? What? What? What if he were to do the same to you when you lead your bulls into the pens?"

"As for Duro," Guilhem admitted, "I know, Ricard, I know very well I had no reason . . ."

"Neither for him nor for the rest," broke in Ricard. "Don't you hear the trumpet? You can say whatever you like, but as long as the fight's not over, your place is in the arena, in the pens, to bring the bulls out."

"Yes, of course," Guilhem protested with his hand up, "you don't have to worry. I left my place, yes; but Bagarro is there, he knows the animals as well as I do. Before the trumpet blast is over, the bull, I'm sure, will be panting already behind the door. It's the same as if I were there myself, don't worry, it's the same."

Ricard snorted. Guilhem's composure irked him.

He took a step forward, got muddied, wiped his shoe in disgust.

Despite the dark and the air currents, despite the coolness of the walls, he was hot now in this enclosed corridor. He stopped, tapped his pale, damp face, and then, furious, unable to stand it any longer, turned his ire against Pavoun.

"In the end, I still don't understand what you're doing here. And, first, what's this nag?"

Guilhem, piqued, shot back.

"This nag, Ricard, is Pavoun."

"What, Pavoun?" retorted Ricard, unfazed by the other's look. "You think maybe I know all the horses bound for the knacker's yard?"

Guilhem, who'd turned white, quickly got hold of himself. "You asked, I answered. It's Pavoun. As you said before, we're not going to have a falling-out over something like that, are we?"

"A falling-out? For that?"

It seemed so absurd to the big man that he burst out laughing. That was a good one! Suddenly smiling, he went back and forth, slapping his thigh and chuckling. The fit of rage spent, he relaxed.

That Guilhem, after all, what a man! Maybe he was going to jump him out of the blue, to attack like a picador!

Still laughing, he stood in front of him.

"It wasn't to hurt you, but after all, I couldn't say he was a thoroughbred."

"Shut up, Ricard, shut up right now!" cried Guilhem, who, in turn, could no longer restrain himself. "He's nothing but a nag, as you can see . . . yes, it's true, nothing but a nag. But to me, no matter what you say, he's Pavoun. Look at this scabby head, this swollen belly, these thighs as see-through as paper. If you'd seen him when he was five, if only you'd seen him! And, I'm not afraid to say, there weren't too many men at the time who could mount him. When I was gardian at Roustan, I was the one who led him by the seden, who strapped on his first saddle. What a horse, my man! People looked at us, you know, when he ran in the ferrado, when he went down the Liço with his white tail flapping against his fetlocks. I wouldn't have traded him, I tell you, for a woman!"

"And yet," Ricard said mockingly, "let's say that Nai . . ."

"There's no Nai or anyone else, I'm telling you. When I saw him just now, lifted up and rolled on the ground, when I thought they would take him back to the bulls, my blood boiled and I left, maddened, for the stalls. Look at him, see what misery!"

"I'm not saying it's not miserable," said Ricard, trying to calm him, "but what do you expect, it's the same for all horses."

"How can you say that, it can't be," cried Guilhem. "The others? Who cares? Do they even know what's in store for them? A nag, though . . . This has to end! You say you were never a gardian, Ricard. You don't know what it is. Come! A Camargue, a horse born in the wild, who knows danger like a man, who, for its whole life, has run with bulls, to drag it out in public with its eyes blindfolded, hitting it with a staff, under the bull's horns? It's a horror that should not be allowed."

Red with rage, choking, he quickly gulped down his saliva; then, his fists in his pockets, he turned, his mind made up, to face Ricard.

"Listen, let's speak plainly, I won't beat around the bush. It's my own fault if I make a fool of myself. Give me the horse, as a friend, for whatever it costs you, and I'll take it back to the manado tonight."

But Ricard calmly protested.

"Look, I don't much understand all this fuss. For me, a nag is a nag, and when an old horse is done for, what's the difference between a bull's horn and a butcher's knife? But as for selling it, my poor Guilhem, I would have a hard time doing that, because it's not mine."

Guilhem made a sign of protest but Ricard went on.

"No, no, the horses here aren't mine; believe me when I tell you. For each fight, it's Bourguin who supplies them. But, after all, what difference does that make? He can't be that far away, I'll have him called. You can come to an understanding with him, you'll see, he's not so bad . . ."

Not much later, Bourguin appeared, wearing espadrilles and armed with a long lance.

As the supplier of horses, he, along with his four brothers, oversaw the hands hired to work in the stalls. On bullfight days, all the Bourguins, fitted out in their filthy trousers and red jackets, flooded the arena. From the start, they swarmed around the picador, following him into the ring, shouting as they prodded horses, sweeping sawdust and sand, unsaddling and covering with heavy canvas the carcasses of dead horses. But it was always Jan Bourguin himself who hung the horns of the dead bull on the front of the chariot while the younger brothers ran beside the mule train in a clamor of ringing bells and cracking whips.

He was approaching with big steps, bustling, breathing heavily. He was hot. Sweat, dark with dust, was streaming down his face and neck.

"Ricard sent me here about the horse . . ."

His breathlessness cut short his words. But he started up again.

"About the horse . . . Listen, Guilhem, work presses. What bedlam, my man! I have to always be in the ring, always running here and there. Well, what do you expect? It's the job."

He wiped his brow with his sleeve, pointed to Pavoun, who, with his muzzle low, seemed asleep on his feet.

"Listen, let's get down to brass tacks. I hear you want to take the horse. You want to take it? Well then, take it!"

He started to guffaw.

"With me, you know, I don't drag things out. That's how it is. It's not to my advantage, as you can imagine, to sell this picador's horse, and if it wasn't for a friend . . ."

He winked.

"Still, you're not getting a bad deal. Clearly the horse is old. You know his age better than I do. But, as a little favor . . ."

He drew closer, dropped his lance, ferreted around in Pavoun's mouth.

"These Camargues, what builds! Look at these teeth. And these legs. It's a creature that could last you another ten years maybe. It's a shame, you rarely see such nags these days. If it weren't for his coat, I wouldn't have him here. But, luckily, the slaughterhouses refuse white animals."

He shrugged, spreading his fingers, as if suddenly seized by fury.

"With their filthy automobiles, it seems, dammit, that horses are over and done with. Oh well! Devil take the hindmost. The more things go on, the more things cost. Soon, we won't be able to make a living. And the price of everything goes up, everything goes up . . ."

Guilhem eyed him warily. What was he getting at? He knew them, this whole pack of horse traders.

"Listen, Bourguin . . ."

The gardian cocked his ear. Over there, in the arena, the death trumpet blared. He was thinking about Nai, in her spot in the stands above the pens, and now he grew impatient.

"Look, you're right, time presses. Tell me, name your price, and if we can, let's get it over with."

"My price? I want to give you a price, but I warn you, it's no use trying to shave off a sou. Listen: the horse is worth fifteen pistoles; for a hundred twenty-five francs, it's yours."

He silenced Guilhem with a gesture.

"There's only one condition: I need the money right away. Oh, don't get upset! This evening, after the fight, whenever you like. But I can't really give you an advance now. Money is too tight. What's more, this is just for a friend, because with all my expenses, this price puts me out of pocket."

He struck a match on the wall and kicked it roughly.

"I tell you, I'm losing. May this cigarette poison me if I'm not speaking the truth."

Guilhem did not say a word. His head down, he seemed to be thinking. A sudden din of music and applause, all the bustle of the arena, did not make him look up.

Nearby, a rough voice rang from the stalls.

"Hey, Bourguin!"

"You see," he said, "they're calling me. What more can I tell you? It will be as you wish. I'll go to the stalls to give the order. So long as there are others, this horse will be spared. Meanwhile, if you decide . . ."

He bent over, took up his lance again, grabbed the horse's bridle. And Guilhem, his jacket on his arm, drew away, watching Bourguin's back grow larger in the light, his receding shadow swaying behind him.

3

Weighed down, Guilhem trudged between the fences. The burning sun dazed him.

The bull lying in the ring, the wild gallop of the mule train, the fluttering up above of fans and umbrellas: it was as if he saw none of it.

Through the stands, the mad cheering spread.

But he went along, head down, bowed under the uproar as if by a blast of mistral.

"Bitch of a life!"

He was thinking only about the condemned animal, the poor horse bound for death in the dark shadows of the stalls.

Oh! If he could have him for five minutes in his hands, that Bourguin, that craven coward, to cram his lies back down his throat!

And then? What good would it do? It was money he needed. Money, right now! Right now!

Unawares, his shoulder brushed the top of the fence, jostling a man who, surprised, began to curse. But a moment later, there were shouts and laughs.

"Well, well! Still this damn Guilhem!"

It was Ricard. Stamping his feet and clapping his hands, he pulled out his handkerchief to wave it. Excited, he suddenly flung his hat over the fences, his straw hat tumbling to the ground. He was cheering the matador at the top of his lungs. His mouth wide open, he was admiring the man's dazzling breast; the sun's bright rays on his gold epaulettes and outspread arms; his brown neck; and his thin torero's pigtail swinging under the knot with each bow.

"A celebrated man, you know!"

He smiled and puffed out his chest in his long jacket.

"Hey, Guilhem, guess how I managed to hire him?"

But, stopping short, he banged the fence with his fist.

"Oh, son of a bitch. What a fool I am! It slipped my mind, I swear, it completely slipped my mind. Well then, how's it going? It didn't work out back there, did it, since you're making such a face?"

Guilhem shook his head.

No, it didn't work out well. Oh! He had to say he was among those that luck never favors. And that Bourguin, that thief Bourguin, for a hundred-franc coin, not to give credit to an honest man who's never harmed anyone in his whole life, a gardian from Arles known to everyone in Provence.

"And for this, Guilhem, you're making yourself so miserable?"

Ricard drew closer, took hold of his sleeve.

"Listen. For your sake, I shouldn't do this. But, after all, it's not just about you. If it makes you happy, here, you'll repay me when you can."

He took out his wallet and rifled through the bills in the thick leather pouch.

"Is this enough? Do you want another fifty ecus?"

But Guilhem, red-faced, sputtered as he refused, the bill fluttering at the tips of his fingers.

"No, no. Go, thank you, this is plenty. Go, Ricard. Thank you! At least, it doesn't put you out, does it?"

His fingers outspread, Ricard gestured broadly with his arm to show him the arena.

"What are you worried about? Forty-sou coins are still raining down here."

Hesitating, Guilhem swayed in place. He would have liked to run.

He longed to be there, to pay, to take hold of Pavoun's filthy reins, this time as master.

The crowd had stopped cheering. The horsemen, lances at their sides, stepped into the arena, returning along the fences to take their places for the fight. In their heavy hats, backsides settled in the saddles, they paraded, weighed down by carapaces of gold braid and glittering sequins.

Loud cheers welcomed their return.

A buzz, a murmur, broken by whistles, echoed through the stands, drowning out the music. Accompanying the sound of popping corks were the cries of men hawking pistachios amid the din.

Any minute now, the trumpet for the bulls would sound.

Guilhem, his mind made up, went toward the pens.

"That's it," cried Ricard, "you have time, but hurry! And above all, hang onto the dough, don't let Nai snatch it."

Not answering, Guilhem laughed as he rushed away.

Nai? A dame? Oh, he had no fear of that.

With money in his pocket now, he felt strong. In one bound, he climbed the little ladder and gaily took off his jacket.

But Bagarro was already there.

Through the noise of locks and slammed doors, crouching or standing, he was cursing, brandishing his trident as he moved across the planks thrown over the pens. A warm dust of rotting wood and old stones thickened the air here, hotter than an oven. Below, despite the light from the opening, every now and then you could barely glimpse, from time to time, a moving neck or back, protruding horns, eyes ablaze in the dark.

A trumpet blast was the signal for the bull's entrance.

The prodded bull arched upward, battered the wooden enclosure, then rushed snorting into the open ring.

Just then, the crowd let out a deafening cheer.

"The devil take us," Bagarro said, "we're dying of heat in here. I'm leaving you to your own devices."

He didn't say another word. He went along the wall, placed his hand on the latch, calmly turned toward Guilhem.

"It's all the same to me, but, next time, when you abandon your place, have the courtesy to at least let someone know. It looks like that Nai has you wrapped around her little finger after all!"

That Nai! That Nai! The fool!

Provoked, he looked at the door Bagarro had just slammed. His back bent, his lips drawn, he sat there motionless, letting his long legs dangle over the pen below. Bagarro's remark got to him. Why was he meddling? Bagarro, Bagarro, the beast! And today of all days, when everything was turning out so well.

Just then, he pulled out his watch. Four o'clock. Good God! And Nai wasn't here. He would never have thought it possible. Quite the opposite—she who would thread her way there on bullfight days, coming secretly to scratch at the door of the pen, so impatient that the overseer, leering at her, had once angrily said to Guilhem, "Here where men work is no place for dames."

The overseer? Bah!

The crowd in the arena was hissing. Frightened, he raised his head.

"Dammit, the horse!"

But there was nothing to fear on that count. Bourguin would not go back on his word. The deal, for him, was a good one. And then, very soon . . .

Again, he pulled out his watch, growing impatient. A low crack, the sound of a nearby horn scraping the planks, made him jump. He cocked his ear: no one. In the end, he drew himself up.

"And then, after all, I'm too foolish!"

Guilhem had known Nai for barely three months. She was from the Cévennes. An orphan, she'd come down from her mountain village at an early age, had been living in Arles for a while.

They'd met for the first time one Sunday during a bullfight.

In charge of a ferrado that day, Guilhem had been leading his horse on foot through the corridor of the stalls when Nai stopped him. What a woman! Her warm beauty, somewhat coarse, had dazzled the gardian at first glance. Red-faced, a little defiant, wary—he'd resisted her flattery. She must be joking—he rode horses like everyone else, doing his job, nothing more. But she, ingratiating, came right up to him, quivering, flashing her teeth, letting the dazed man smell the fragrance of her bodice.

They'd spoken again since then. She kept him bound.

When, during the day, his staff in hand, alone in the vast countryside, he prodded his bulls; or when, at dusk, in front of the cabins, he watched the moon rise as bitterns called, he no longer thought of anything but Nai.

Everything about her enchanted him.

To be able to live with her, he would have borne work, a shop—in a word, the town's slavery. He would have left his gardian's life.

But she, when he first spoke of it, had cried out.

"You're mad, my poor Guilhem. Do you think you'd please me if you were a mechanic or laborer? What fools men are! Oh well . . ."

He hadn't insisted. All women are a little mad. This one loved men who tended bulls, that was her passion.

Still, deep down, he was glad. What then would stop Nai from joining him in the Camargue? The bulls, the horses on the manado, the huge wild sansouiro would keep her busy for a while. She could take care of Pavoun. That good-for-nothing would definitely improve in the countryside, and, as Bourguin said, for a tiny little favor . . .

Despite the din outside, despite the cries and the music, Guilhem gradually dozed off in the stifling heat of the pens.

A wave of whistling, some louder yells, made him sometimes rock gently from left to right. He was almost dreaming. Visions drifted through his sleep, mingling pell-mell in his head: the cabin over there and Nai, Pavoun, Pavoun . . .

This time, by God, someone had knocked.

He found himself standing upright behind the door, blinking, dazed, his eyes still swollen, greeting Nai who'd just come in.

"Oh, well, it's not so bad! Are you just getting here?"

She said not a word. Swaying in place, scratching the damp, crumbling wall with the tip of her umbrella, it seemed she was afraid to go up the ladder by herself. Sullen, her brows furrowed under her curls, she was staring at Guilhem in a way he'd never seen.

More than usual, now, she looked beautiful. Enthralled, he gazed at her, trying to make out her supple body in the darkness: her breasts, her thighs, her arms quivering under her white dress.

They could shout all they wanted to over there, all of them. He didn't hear them.

To tease her, he started to laugh.

"You don't look too happy, do you, Nai?"

Happy. Just the word made her explode.

Happy, that was a good one. Oh, well, of course she couldn't complain, it was too bad, too bad. Who knew what it was like for a woman like her to be mixed up with a gardian?

She broke off to sneer.

A gardian, that was saying too much. A Bohemian, rather, a sort of Caraco; wasn't he planning to trade in picadors' old horses?

"Are you a fool? You! Buy a nag? Are you rolling in dough or what?"

He protested with a gesture.

"It must be a joke after all. What's this I hear about Pavoun-Blanc? To pick a fight, to go into debt, for an animal? I was on my way here, people called me, they stopped me to tell me this, and you want me to be happy? You dare to lead onto the manado such a nag, a ninny of a wreck, good only to rot in a hole?"

"For God's sake," said Guilhem, "tongues do wag. I had some plans, yes, I'm not saying I didn't. But before going into debt, Nai, listen, I can think it over again, and if it causes you so much pain . . ."

He swayed and leaned toward her with a warm look to appease her, taking hold of her two wrists and laughing . . .

"After the bullfight, little one . . ."

A heavy knock rattled the door; Bagarro's voice boomed.

"Hey, Guilhem, are you ready?"

In the stands, amid shouts, murmurs, and cheers, whistles dominated.

"In God's name!"

Below, the picadors were in their saddles. In a cloud of dust, the mule train was dragging the dead bull.

Guilhem got busy. And Nai? Had she left? Oh well, she'd return. Women had to be led. "Not too rough, just soft enough." A good saying. He'd settle the affair and Nai need know nothing about it. It wasn't that hard. Nai? If he wanted, he could make her believe that pigs fly.

The trumpet sounded, the iron clanged. Bent over the pens, Guilhem used both hands to prick the bull, then watched as, head down in the dark corridor, it suddenly vanished toward the light.

Panting, he ran to the opening. It was urgent. Where was he now, that Bourguin?

The bull, limp, refused the pic this time, and the banderilleros, amid hisses, flanked the picador and little by little cornered the beast to make it charge.

Irked, Guilhem shook his head. In front of him, down below, he could see the blue shirt, the carpenter's back. Furious, the man was whistling with two fingers stuck in his mouth.

"Pack of ninnies!"

But the shouts, dying out, were suddenly hushed. The bull, halfhearted at first, heated up when it tasted the iron. Enraged by the lance that had pierced its neck from its muzzle to its shank, it butted the man. The horse, caught by its straps, was lifted up and shaken like a dead carcass, then thrown onto its back on the sand.

"Hey Guilhem!"

Despite the cheers and clamor, stunned, he turned his head. It was Nai, back again, this time readily setting her foot on the boards.

"Listen . . ."

He noticed the hoarse voice, the slightly trembling mouth.

"You'll give it to me, your money, all of it. I know, I know . . ."

Out of breath, she paused. Too much anger was choking her. With her crumpled handkerchief, she wiped her lips, white under the faded red.

"All the money, now! What? Don't lie to me, it's not worth the trouble. You didn't say anything, by God, so you could cheat me. Oh, you filthy man!"

Raising her voice, beside herself, she was almost shouting.

"You don't want to? You don't want to? You can keep it, you're free. But know, you'll pay in the end, you can count on it. You'd better choose."

She came close, spat in his face.

"I've had enough. Take your nag, but afterward don't ever talk to me again, it would do you no good, I won't answer. You can look at me all you want, you still don't know me. You don't know who I am. I'll see you die at my feet, I'll crush you without looking back. You know it now, make up your mind, I'll never forget! Never!"

As she slammed the door, she repeated, "Never!"

Left alone there, stunned, he turned his back to the arena.

Never? Never? The bitch! She'd do that to him. What a look, really, on her face, and those tight fists and eyes. Her eyes. The hot voice came back to him, burning with rage. She wasn't joking, that was sure. But really, what did she want? Pavoun was just an excuse. She wanted to rule the man, she wanted to be right. He knew dames well! So, they'd have to part . . .

Worried, he took off his hat, scratched his head. Too many thoughts swirled at once in his brain. The noise of the arena flustered him.

Would they have to part over this?

Drifting through the odor of dirt and dung that rose from the depths of the pen, a whiff of Nai's scent came to him. He breathed it in greedily. He thought he could see all of her. In the doorway of her house, in the darkness of the staircase, in her room over there in La Rouqueto: it was that scent, time after time, that came to him. It was the smell of her dresses, her pillow, her white lace. A confused longing made him limp.

He knew very well, by God, that a woman like that was too good for him, it couldn't last. Well then, it was over, and that was that. That was that.

His hands over his ears, he stood straighter so he could think. Maybe, after all, he was moving too fast. Why lose his head? If she didn't care, Nai wouldn't be raging like this. It was clear. She'd attacked him because she was attached to him.

He stretched his neck, blinked his eyes.

Also, on this matter, maybe Nai had a point. This Pavoun, it hurt to watch him die in the arena. But what could he do about it?

Even buying him would do no good. Everyone was right. He was nothing but a nag. The animal was nearing its end. He might drag on for a while, trailing his old bones on the manado, but then, one fine day, he'd rot in the brackish water and mud on the edge of a lagoon. She was right. Oh, misery! Did he need to go into debt for that?

The crowd's howls were louder than the trumpet's call. *Hou hou hou . . . !* From all sides, with great shouts, they were crying.

"No banderillas! Pic! Pic! Horses, horses!"

His temples on fire, Guilhem shook his head.

"And yet, my poor Pavoun . . ."

Suddenly straightening up, he leapt back angrily, one hand in his pocket, fingering Ricard's money.

"And so, will I let this happen for a dame?"

He rallied. Nai? Well! Too bad for her.

He was no longer wavering. He'd go and pay, take the horse, be done with it once and for all. Later, surely, they'd be happy.

Quick-quick, straddling the fence, he placed his foot on the ladder.

"Damn!"

He stood still, eyes on the arena, staring at the horse door. He was too late. Pavoun was coming out of the stalls, trotting under the great saddle, spurred by Duro, who was on top of him. With one hand, an attendant pulled him by the bit; with the other he prodded his croup with a stick. The horse was trembling. At the top of his bloody leg, the wound had opened again. His ears tense and his eyes blindfolded, he stumbled along the fence, frozen with fear.

"Hey, toro!"

At the man's voice, the bull turned. He was scratching the sand, already angered by the pics, watching this mass of red and gold, whose smell alone drove him wild, come toward him, growing larger under the dark caparison.

When it was beside him, he suddenly turned his horns and prepared to charge.

The crowd, for an instant, was still.

In the silence you could hear the clash of a lance, Duro's hoarse voice challenging the bull.

"Hey, toro!"

And, so as not to see any more, Guilhem briefly lowered his head and, with both hands in front of his eyes, made as if to light his pipe under his hat brim.

The Longline

1

To the north of the old roubino, behind the cabin at Claus-Brula, was an abyss. It was a big hole filled with thick water and mud, which the animals rarely visited, and on whose salt-ravaged sandy rim no grass ever grew.

Every day before dawn, Pèire Gargan stood on the doorstep of his cabin and looked up to check the weather; then, with his rope slung over his shoulder, he left to round up his horses scattered across Claus-Brula. Riding bareback all morning, he combed through the woods and the samphire; all morning, his sharp voice could be heard along the margins, chiding stragglers: "He! Hehe! Hou!" But as soon as the sun reached nine o'clock and the gathered animals were splashing in the marsh, the gardian returned to his spot under an arching juniper that gave some shade not far from the big hole.

Stretched out on his belly, his head between his fists, or propped on his long gardian's staff, he liked to stay there for hours on end to watch the fish swim up, swift shadows that darted from the depths and skimmed the surface of the old abyss, which, quivering, seemed to wake up and come to life.

"What bitches!"

No question about it: there were mullet here, fat as thighs it seemed, that he would never taste.

In a big hole like this, where two horsehair ropes tied end to end and weighted with a heavy stone could not touch bottom, the fish vanished at the slightest sign.

The lowered trap whose tight sides steadily enclose the fish; the lines secretly, slowly dropped; the baskets carefully placed at night in the glow of dusk—Gargan had tried everything.

Lucky for him, there were eels. Through the deep water and mud, they gamboled freely in the darkness. And when, in the evening, he attached several hooks to the same cord and threw his longline into the abyss, in the morning he could count on pulling out at least two or three of those eels with their white bellies and greenish heads the color of the sea—eels whose flesh, in a *catigot*, melts in your mouth like marrow.

Thin-skinned and fiercely jealous about his fishing, Gargan never visited his neighbors. But sometimes, as he rounded up his animals on the far reaches, he met men from Lansa or Galejoun.

"Hey, Pèire Gargan, how's your longline doing?"

"Not bad, my friend."

"And when will you give us a taste of your eels?"

"If you bring along a bottle, my good man, you can come whenever you like."

Of an evening, then, you'd see a few pairs of horsemen trotting briskly on the sansouiro. From far away, they hailed each other. Bottles poked out of their sacks. Pèire Gargan went to light his fire, wash the dishes, rinse the glasses; then all night long, till very late, they carried on *à la gardiano* in front of steaming plates piled high with slices of eel redolent of garlic, saffron, and pure wine.

*   *   *

When he went to toss his longline one evening, Pèire Gargan had a shock. On the soft sand margin where no one usually came, he saw tracks he didn't recognize. They were the prints of heavy feet, the thick soles of a man who'd squatted there, leaving these traces of his body's weight in the mud.

Someone had come here! Who? Dammit! He was gripped by anxiety.

That, in this vast countryside, someone would even cross Claus-Brula! Except for neighboring gardians, whoever came through already counted as an intruder, unwelcome. But that anyone had the gall to ruin his fishing, to come and traipse around the hole? Some poacher, most likely, scrounging around the lagoons . . .

With his teeth clenched, he bent over, carefully lowered his line, then returned, grumbling, to his cabin. The next day, when he went out before dawn, he took a detour. In the pale emerging light, the jumbled tracks from the previous night could still be seen, along with the thin line that stretched, gray and muddy like a worm in the dark water.

"It's still early," Gargan said, "we'll see better later."

And when the sun was high, when the slaked horses, their bells ringing, turned toward the flowing waters of Bras-Mort to graze in the reeds, the gardian went again to the roubino.

An obsession held him; he did not move very fast. Watchful, he rocked on his legs, eyeing the sea purslane and samphire around him.

But suddenly enraged, he bent down, dropped his staff, and in one bound reached the abyss.

"Damned luck!"

On the disturbed sand, like the night before, big feet had left their prints; the margin was sticky with mud; the longline was gone.

"Goddamn luck!"

Trembling, he studied this new slap in the face: mixed in with the footprints, here, not long ago, some fine eels had been dragged. He kneeled, scratched with his nail, took up a pinch of sand: it sparkled in the sun on his half-open palm. This was the worst! Scales, mullet scales, for God's sake! Gripped by a cold fury, he gnashed his teeth and howled. Mullet! It had been years since he, Gargan, had caught anything other than eels, and now some filthy tramp, some son of a bitch, had come here by highways and byways to steal Claus-Brula's mullet from under his nose! And, what was even worse, with his own longline! The bastard!

Emboldened, he reclaimed his staff and rushed to the woods, following the tracks.

But beyond the sandy border, the dry earth was so hard, all cracked by heat, that no track remained.

Here and there, a bush crushed by a passing animal; a hole gouged during the rains by a stallion's hoof or mares on the run; the lair of a surprised rabbit that had fled zigzagging through the sansouiro.

Nothing more.

So Gargan returned, eyed the sand and the dark water again, stood there thinking. The sun was growing less hot. The usual time for lunch and siesta had passed. But lost in thought, he saw nothing, neither his shadow lengthening on the sand nor his horses, which, escaping into the rice paddies, were wildly racing past the borders of Bras-Mort.

* * *

Ever since the longline had been stolen, the eel thief seemed to have disappeared.

Each evening, once his lamp was lit, while the little pot came to a boil, Gargan went to the abyss and dropped his line for the night, but he never again saw a man's tracks on the sand, neither when he left at daybreak nor when he returned to the juniper for his midday rest. It became a memory that, without worrying him too much, mingled from time to time with the delirium of dreams during his light naps.

Someone had come here, that was certain. And so? Some lost traveler, most likely, ravaged by hunger, who must be far away by now.

He'd have to be a fool to still be worried about it.

When this thought came to him in his half-sleep, he turned over, laughed to himself, shrugged, and, momentarily reassured, rolled into the shade so he could sleep better.

On this day, waking early, Gargan half-opened his eyelids and saw something dark, huddled barely a few feet in front of him.

He raised his head abruptly.

Shocked, he made out the back, the filthy pants, the grease-stained hat of a man squatting near the abyss.

"The tramp!"

His eyes still swollen with sleep, he stood up and quietly, quickly, took off his shoes.

Despite his trembling body and the blood pounding in his veins, he moved forward with small steps, striking the earth with his staff as he stepped over the samphire. "We'll see, we'll see now."

Unawares, he snapped a twig under his bare foot, crushed some sod as he scaled a small mound.

But the other man did not move. His hand high, his neck long, he had his eye on the cork bobbing in the middle of the hole, at the end of a line suspended from a little stick.

Gargan could no longer stand it; he hurried around and stood in front of him.

"Hey, you!"

His hands clutching his staff, his voice croaking, he was enraged to see two mullet on the ground, bellies up, still twitching.

"Hey you, who said you could fish here?"

The man, unperturbed, as if deaf, casually pulled in his line, grabbed his bait, threaded a fat earthworm onto the point of the hook, then dropped the stick, and suddenly turned, head down, to rush at Pèire Gargan.

The attack was soon over.

The gardian, surprised, had rolled. If he hadn't pulled away, he would have been slammed right in the stomach. Instead, badly shaken by a kick to his back, he got to his knees just as the other man, thinking he was down, lunged at him with a knife. Pèire Gargan had not let go of his staff during his tumble, and, in a great turnabout, holding it now at arm's length, he bashed in the tramp's forehead.

* * *

It had already been three days since the body had sunk into the abyss. Pèire Gargan was unconcerned.

When he'd seen the tramp laid low on the sand, he had not thought he'd killed him; these brutes have a hard life: this one would heal from the cudgel's blow all by himself in the night's cool.

But when he rose in the early morning and found the body stiff, the four limbs already frozen, he had to face facts: the tramp was definitely dead.

And so? He'd shrugged. It wasn't that bad. They needed more such deaths, to cleanse the land of its rabble. Better him than me.

And to think that without his staff, he might have been there, stretched out like carrion. He felt no pity. Again he saw the man crouched down, scowling under his reddish beard, his head barreling forward, charging with his brow like a bull. What filth!

But still, what was he going to do about it?

Little by little, the dawning day made the water in the hole sparkle with reflections of a cloudless sky. Already the east was reddening and any minute now the sun would rise.

Gargan made up his mind. He leapt onto the embankment by the roubino and turned in all directions to check the horizon. Then he went back to the tramp, took hold of his feet, and dropped him into the abyss.

He'd felt at ease for three days.

Whistling, he'd leave in the morning and scour the countryside to round up his mares. He was alone again; he was master. He could come and go as he pleased, without feeling around him the hostile presence that haunted him; he would never again see the tramp's big tracks on the sansouiro!

Still, more than before, he liked to stay close to the cabin, and, when siesta-time came, he no longer went to lie down in front of the big hole as before. He remained where he was, leaning on his staff, dreaming and watching the clouds go by.

"O Gargan, are you asleep on your feet?"

It was Master Galino, from the Lansa manado. The little old man, in his saddle, was laughing out loud, his mouth stretched all the way to his white sideburns. Gargan jumped.

"See that now? If I were a constable, I'd think you had a guilty conscience. What are they up to, your mares?"

As he answered, Gargan forced a laugh.

"The mares are fine, Master Galino, there's plenty of good grass here. But it's not my mares you're looking for in all this sun, is it?"

"Not at all, not at all!"

Galino dismounted, explained matters.

Tomorrow he was expecting the impresario from Narbouno, to sell him some bulls. The man was a big eater and drinker, and he loved fish. In the morning, he'd naturally eat at Lansa, but Galino had also promised him that, for supper, he would bring him to Claus-Brula for some bouillabaisse in the cabin.

"And so, you understand, your longline . . ."

Gargan suddenly turned white.

The longline? Yes, yes . . . well, he didn't know. What with the days lengthening, he had to linger later with the animals. And then, despite his efforts, the eels were hardly biting. But, still, yes, of course, if he had time . . .

Laughing, Galino clapped him on the shoulder.

"Hey, you fool, are you upset about this? You don't have time? I'll send someone to lower your longline for you."

But Gargan hastily cried out.

"No, no, Master Galino, don't worry, no matter what, I'll take care of it. I was just saying . . . don't worry. Send someone for so little? I know you must be joking. The longline? It will be lowered."

And as the other was already heading off, swaying in his saddle, Gargan wiped his brow and called out even louder.

"Count on it Master Galino, don't send anyone, it will be lowered!"

2

The gardian, his door shut, was moving down the embankment.

The damp sansouiro shone, and the clumps of samphire, growing larger in the darkness, seemed to be a flock of sheep, dozing in the moonlight. Not a sound could be heard in the calm night. Only, from time to time, a fox yelped as it hunted in the woods, or a bull's bell rang on the strand.

For the first time in his life, the silence weighed on Pèire Gargan.

He trembled.

Why did he have to go out at this hour? Those *coulau* from Lansa could very well leave him alone. They? How could they have guessed that a dead man was rotting in the muck of the abyss? A dead man!

Again, he shuddered. He had the urge to flee ahead of time, to run from the cabin. But then what? He wasn't going to scare himself, after all, was he? To believe in ghosts and revenants, to be frightened like a woman?

He held onto his rope more firmly and continued along the embankment, not looking up until he reached the rim of the hole.

But suddenly he was so stunned he staggered and nearly fell. Everything started to spin around him—water, sky, sansouiro. He was dazed by dizziness.

Oh! There! . . . There! On the still water, the tramp's drowned face!

The tramp?—Returning!

He got down on his knees, a frozen sweat streaming down his spine; he was suffocating. He no longer thought of fleeing. All the terror of the night, the dead man, the emptiness—all of it together crushed him.

And so? He had, after all, found him here. He'd thrown him into the abyss, he was sure of it. And so?

By God! Now, little by little, he understood. The corpse, as it rotted, had come up to the water's surface. He understood.

But his fever did not abate.

All of a sudden, fear of the living thrust aside fear of the dead. Tomorrow, some lost hunter, some patrolling guard passing the hole would come and see the floating carcass; people would speak of it everywhere; he'd be accused.

At this thought, he jumped to his feet. He set off running down the path.

When he returned, out of breath, with a heavy stone on his shoulder, the moon was setting. It was late. It had been quite a job, to carry to the hole this block of sandstone, which, right by the door, had served to sharpen knives. It was late. With the end of his staff, he pushed the body onto the sand. Now, he'd better hurry.

But as he handled the tramp, he trembled with fear and loathing. A smell of silt and rot sickened him. The water, the night air, made his hands as stiff as the swollen hands of the corpse.

He could not take any more.

As he set one leg into the loop of the slipknot, something quick wound under the thick, velvety muck. It was an eel, most likely, starting in on the dead man's belly. It twisted around slyly, came out from under the shirt, flashed its shining back and flat head, then soundlessly dove into the hole. At that moment, the stone slipped along the sand, dragging the body, which sank into the depths of the gulf.

*　*　*

The rest of the night, until dawn, he had not been able to shut his eyes. Then he started to rave in a riot of specters and horrors, caught in a feverish torpor that kept him from rising, no matter how hard he tried.

He was shivering.

At one moment, he thought he was sinking, his body bloated and his feet heavy, into the muck of the abyss; at another, as in the fight, the tramp was attacking him: the man leapt, his eyes dull, his hair muddy, and Gargan felt a great blow to his belly, a shock that unnerved him. He ended up awake with cramps in his guts; the blow must have really injured him.

Struggling against dizziness, he finally stood up, held onto the walls to reach the jar, gulped down the pitcher of stale water, consumed by a dog's thirst. But he was forgetting his trouble.

The tramp, over there, rotting in the abyss; it was he, Gargan, who'd killed him!

Ever since he'd seen the body, tied to the sandstone, sink into the hole, this specter had haunted him—the scummy beard; the fingers; the bloated paunch under the slimy velvet of the filthy pants; and the eyes, above all the eyes, the dreadful eyes of the dead.

A trembling shook him. All day long, he shivered as he dragged himself from his bed to his door. Wrapped in his burnoose, he sat for a long time in the sun, sheltered by his cabin. Nothing could warm him.

He had killed. He thought of nothing else. He had killed. A man's life, a life for a longline.

The longline! Despite his weakness, exhausted, he got up. Hou! He remembered. The longline. The overseer Galino was coming with the others for supper. And so? If they didn't find fish here, if the bouillabaisse hadn't been made . . . He would go, he'd go himself! To think of those people, mucking about in the abyss . . .

God help him. They would wonder . . .

The fear that until then had beaten him down suddenly revived him, set him back on his feet. He took charge. He was hot. His blood flowed once more under his skin, burning like fire.

He grabbed his hat and his gardian's staff, left for the hole. He would have liked to have run. But his head was still spinning, and he tottered on his limp legs at almost every step.

"I'll get there soon, by God!"

A foul smell chased him. Just to think of the muck rekindled his fever. He thought of nothing but the longline, the eels in the big hole, the greedy beasts slowly snaking around the corpse in the mud.

* * *

Suddenly a great sound of voices, a trampling on the sansouiro could be heard. It was a group of horsemen arriving. All four dismounted and encircled a man in a long alpaca jacket, his belly spilling over the front of his saddle.

"You can come down, Mister Maliver!"

As he got out of the stirrups, the man, tangled in the mane, brought his leg heavily over the neck of the old horse they were holding by the bridle, just in case. Galino had crossed the threshold.

"Gargan, this is Mister Maliver, impresario at Narbouno."

But when Galino glimpsed Pèire's face, he suddenly cried out.

"What's wrong with you, my good man? Have you caught some bad marsh fever?"

They would see. He, Galino, knew about these things.

With his thumb, he pulled back an eyelid and inspected the gardian like a horse.

"Do you see that vein in his eye? With men, Mister Maliver, it's the same as with animals."

He forced him to sit back down. No one should work when they're sick. There were plenty of men around the fire.

To clean the eels, Galino rolled them with his feet in the sand; in the little pan, chopped onions, browning in oil, mingled their fragrance with garlic and bay.

"It will be some bouillabaisse!"

Maliver was ecstatic. He'd never visited a cabin before.

The slanting reed roof with its willow beams, the white roughcast, the horns hung on the walls with sedens and saddles, all of it, all of it thrilled him. He struck his big paunch.

"Oh, if only I'd known this as a young man, I'd have made a great gardian!"

They all laughed.

They were at table. For a moment, the men's chatter dispelled Pèire Gargan's torment. More or less fasting since the night before, he suddenly felt his appetite return in front of the golden broth and bread.

"Eat, have some bouillabaisse, Mister Maliver!"

Louder than the others, Maliver's voice thundered.

"When you come to Narbouno . . . I think I've chosen a nice lot of bulls for my arena . . . What do you say, Master Galino, about the little black one who was giving the horses the evil eye?"

Slurping the soup, he turned.

"You, fevered man, taste this, to chase the bile!"

With the tip of his knife, he thrust two chunks of eel onto Gargan's bread. They were nice and round, warm and shining with sauce. But, as he stuck his fork into them, Pèire suddenly turned white. The specter returned: the tramp, the blow with the staff, the sandstone rolled into the abyss. He had killed. This cooked animal, right under his nose, sickened him. Horrified, he kept seeing the one just like it, the one he'd seen slip out from under the shirt, the one that all night long had nibbled the tramp's stinking flesh.

"Are you all right, Pèire?"

He was leaning on his elbows, his teeth clattering, not seeing a thing.

Frozen stiff, he nearly fainted.

The others had to put him to bed. And to restore him, Master Galino, who knew cures, had him swallow a big glass of boiling-hot wine, spiked with sage and a head of dried pepper.

* * *

On horseback with his nephew, Master Galino was shouting as he chased mares across Claus-Brula. As they pursued each other, a great train of animals galloped down the embankment in a clamor of bells. Suddenly neighing, a stallion laid down his ears and bit a croup or kicked the sides of a foal as he flew by.

The baile of Lansac could not help laughing.

"This stolen grass is good for them. They're too fat, the bitches! They think only of playing."

But the other man, galloping along the ditch, angrily complained.

"Pack of lice! Sick or not, I'm going to speak to Gargan. For days now, these mares have been despoiling us. It's been weeks they've been leading us in a chase. It's time for this to stop, once and for all!"

To tell the truth, Gargan hardly went out. Now and then he got up, painfully hoisting himself onto his horse, doing his gardian's work. But he was so tired at night he had to lie down again before dusk, and the next day he didn't have the strength to start over.

The mares, neglected, wandered at will, breaking all bounds, drawn to the open spaces or the neighbors' grass.

Master Galino was aware of it, and when he sometimes met them on his land, he got on his horse and brought them back without a word.

"Listen," he said gently, "what's a little grass between neighboring manados? It's not a problem. Let's not bother Gargan now, he's too sick. When I met him the other day, talking to himself like a madman by the abyss, I tried to joke: 'Hey, how's it going, your longline?' But he suddenly backed away, his legs gave out, and he fell onto a clump of samphire. I thought he'd fainted. He must be very sick. Do you know what I'm afraid of? That he has brain fever."

The nephew did not answer.

He was riding a small, skittish horse that was tossing its head and snorting without stop in its cabassoun. Concerned about this animal struggling in its straps, he had little pity for Pèire Gargan's sickness. Sick? He knew about those fevers! Only good-for-nothings were sick. What gardian, in such weather, would not have been able to round up his animals? And so? Each man for himself.

The sun was beating down. The mares, smelling the fresh grass, were now heading straight for the marsh. Midday was coming. A warm, brisk air was rising like fire from the sansouiro, making the salt pools and distant waters of Bras-Mort shimmer.

"Good," said Galino, "now we can finish our siesta. Come, what are you looking at out there?"

Surprised, the overseer leaned toward the boy who was lagging behind, his eyes lost in the sansouiro.

"I can't see a thing."

But right away he caught himself.

"Hey, what the devil, what's going on in the Claus-Brula abyss?"

"With such disorder here, it's no surprise to see foals floating," the other man answered. "If Gargan won't herd, plenty more will die."

"That's no foal," Galino said.

Heading straight for the abyss along the path, they left at a great trot. But they could make out nothing. The sun, reflecting off the placid water, blinded them; the fiery air blurred everything; and the horses' brusque movements made some sort of black mass, shapeless in all this glare, dance before their eyes.

"That's no foal," Master Galino repeated.

Suddenly, he grabbed his hat, spurred his horse, leaned over, and, with three kicks, crossed the sansouiro at a gallop. But when he reached the rim, he recognized Pèire Gargan, blanched and bloated, half eaten by eels, floating in his shirt in the middle of the hole.

AUTHOR'S NOTES

These notes were prepared by Jóusè d'Arbaud and included in the 1926 bilingual edition of *La Bèstio dóu Vacarés / La Bête du Vaccarès* and in the 1929 bilingual edition of *La Caraco / Raconte Camarguen*. In the main text, words from the Provençal language are italicized on first use in each story; here, italics are used to indicate the word or phrase being glossed.

The Beast of Vacarés

Lou Vacarés. The Vaccarès. The biggest lagoon in the Camargue, so named because of the herds of wild cows that graze along its borders. Root: *vaca*. Low Latin: *Vacaresium*. The transcription Valcarès, often used, is incorrect.

Notice

3   *Manado*. Free-ranging herd of bulls or wild horses. The *manado* is managed by a *baile* or overseer, who has under his command *gardians* or comrades.

3   *Lou Grand-Rose*. The Great Rhône. The Rhône, at Arles, divides into two branches to form the Camargue delta: the Great Rhône that runs into the sea at Port-Saint-Louis, and the Little Rhône, whose mouth is at Grau d'Orgon, very close to Les Saintes-Maries-de-la-Mer.

3   *Camargo*. The Camargue. The present-day delta has an area of some 75,000 hectares. But the name "Camargue" is actually applied to the group of salt flats that form the ancient delta, including both the Little Camargue near Aigues-Mortes in the west, and the great and little Plan-du-Bourg, near Fos in the east. The total area of this alluvial plain is 130,000 hectares.

3   *Roubino*. Canal, large irrigation ditch.

3   *Estanié*. Provençal cabinet, built especially to hold dishes and tin utensils.

3   *Tamarisso*. Tamarisk. Tree in the *Tamaricaceae* family, very common in the Camargue and along the entire Mediterranean coast.

3   *Catigot*. A sort of bouillabaisse made with wine, one of the most typical Camargue dishes.

4 *Bouvino.* Bulls. Collective name for animals of the bovine species, and, particularly, the herds of wild bulls in the Camargue.

First Chapter

6 *Nosto-Damo-de-la-Mar.* Our Lady of the Sea. The current village of Les Saintes-Maries-de-la-Mer in the Camargue, known for its fortified basilica, around which the annual pilgrimage of the 24th and 25th of May attracts the Gypsies, was once called *Vilo-de-la-Mar* or *Nostra-Dona-de-la-Mar*, and, in low Latin, *Sancta Maria de Mari, Sancta Maria de Ratis.* According to tradition in Arles, this is where the three Marys and several disciples landed after the death of Christ.

6 *Lou Riege.* The Riège. Woods formed by a group of small islands in the southern part of the Vacarés lagoon. They are also called: the woods of Eriège, the Reiriège, Riruge, or Reiruge.

6 *Roussatino.* Collective name designating all the horses of the Camargue race, or *rosso, rosses.* Note that this word in its Provençal usage does not contain the pejorative sense of the French word *rosse* ("bitch") and remains quite close to its Germanic root: *ross,* horse. The Camargue horse, whose type is quite distinct, is considered to be a species very little evolved from the prehistoric Salutrean race.

6 *La Séuvo.* The Sylve. Region of the Camargue, once very wooded, formed from an old sandbar. Sylve-Réal (*Sylva Regalis*) is on the Little Rhône; Sylve Godesque (*Sylva Gothica*) near Aigues-Mortes. In the Sylve Godesque, a votive altar was discovered, dedicated to the god Sylvanus for the benefit of a herd of livestock:

SILVANO

VOTVM. PRO

ARMENTO

6 *Saumòdi.* Psalmody. Old Benedictine abbey near Aigues-Mortes.

7 *Ficheiroun.* Trident, the weapon of the bull gardian. The trident consists of an iron lance with three points shaped like a half moon, set on a chestnut haft about two meters long. Among themselves, gardians call it *lou ferre,* the iron.

7 *Draio.* Rural path where flocks have the right to pass, especially during transhumance.

8 *Restencle.* Mastic. Shrub, a sort of pistachio.

8 *Óulivastre* or *daladèu.* Alaternus (buckthorn). Evergreen shrub, common to the Riege woods.

8 *Mourven.* Phoenician juniper.

8   *Tiragasso. Tiragasse.* Mediterranean smilax or rough bindweed, also called *arriège, arieuge, saliège*. It is to this prickly vine that the Riège woods evidently owes its name: *Bos d'Ariège*, called *Ariège*, or *d'Ariuege*.

8   *La Vièio ié danso.* The Old Dancer. The way people in the Camargue refer to mirages. Mirages are common in the Camargue, especially around the Vacarés. They begin with a vibration in the air, a trembling that runs along the ground and seems to make the images dance; it spreads into the distance in great waves that reflect the dark thickets. How not to see in this mysterious *Vièio*, dancing in the desert sun, a folk memory of the untouchable wild goddess, ancient power, spirit of solitude, once considered divine, that remains the soul of this great wild land?

8   *Primaio.* The "prime" birds, whose arrival occurs first, *à primo*, in other words, in springtime.

8   *Baisso.* Depression of the earth, often quite extended, where the fresh water that remains during the rainy season spawns a marshy vegetation that attracts wildfowl.

8   *Gaso.* Ford. Safe passage through the quicksand or lagoons.

8   *Sansouiro.* Uncultivated mudflat. More particularly, the surface of sterile, bare land, covered with efflorescences of salt during the dry season.

10 *Rasclet.* Little rail, marsh bird.

10 *Vibre.* Beaver. The Rhône *vibre*. Low Latin: *veber*; Latin: *fiber*.

13 *Bon-Pache.* Good pact. A gardian's nickname.

16 *Seden.* Braided horsehair rope, used in the Camargue as a lasso and halter. The seden is part of the harness of "bull horses"; folded in half, knotted at the neck at one end, it is twisted around the saddle's pommel at the other. The gardians themselves make it with horsehair of different colors, whose combinations allow them to vary the decorative trappings.

16 *Quatren.* Four-year-old colt. At one year old, the colt is called *court*; at two, *doublen*; at three, *ternen*.

17 *Dèstre.* Right side. To lead a horse *en dèstre* is to lead it by hand.

17 *Largado.* The western wind. Gardians typically orient themselves by the wind, and often designate their directions with the name of the wind.

17 *Cabassoun.* A sort of metal muzzle with articulated points that encloses the horse's nose during training. In the Camargue, the cabassoun is used with braided horsehair reins that cross and fall on either side of the neck. The horse is first fitted with a cabassoun with reins and a bridle bit. Once the training is over, the cabassoun is removed and the animal is afterwards governed solely with the bridle reins.

17 *Lunèu.* Lunel in Languedoc.

23 *Calèu*. Little oil lamp with an antique shape, generally triangular, in metal. A strip with a hook allows it to be suspended in the hearth or in an angle of the chimney.

25 *Se desbrandant*. Defending himself. *Desbrandage* is a series of violent bucks, rapid and repeated, peculiar to Camargue horses.

Second Chapter

32 *Nègo-Biòu*. Bull-Drowner. The name of a gaso or ford in the Riege.

32 *Mourraioun*. Muzzle with reins, formed with the seden or horsehair rope, to replace the bridle when one rides bareback.

32 *Béu-l'òli*. Oil-drinker. Barn owl, nocturnal bird. *Strix flammea*, so called in Provence because people believe it enters churches at night to drink oil from lamps.

42 *Eimargue, Queilar, Galargue, Vau-verd*. Place-names in Languedoc.

45 *Brouqueto*. Stick or piece of hemp soaked at one end in sulfur or tallow and used to carry fire from coals in the hearth.

The Caraco

51 *Gounflo-Anguielo*. Eel-blower. A gardian's surname. The reader should note once and for all that none of the names or surnames used here refer to any actual persons, living or dead, in the Camargue.

51 *Radèu*. Sandy islet emerging from the water of the lagoons or from the dry mudflats.

51 *Roubino*. Irrigation ditch.

51 *Clamadou*. Name of a deserted area in the Little Camargue between the Rhône and Aigues-Mortes, always occupied by herds of wild bulls. Roman: *Clamador*.

51 *Queilar*. Area in Low Languedoc where a certain number of herds come, through immemorial rights of transhumance, to spend the summer months. Queilar is thus an important bullfighting center.

51 *Bouveau*. Enclosures for bulls, built from palisades when they are fixed and with open fencing when they are moveable. The *bouveau* serve to enclose the manado's bulls each evening, and to perform some pastoral operations. Root: *Bovis*.

52 *Grand-Radèu*. The name of an area in the Little Camargue.

52 *Caraco*. A "Bohemian" or Gypsy. In the Camargue and Languedoc, this is the name given to the nomadic Romani people whose patron is Saint Sara and who come each year, the 24th and 25th of May, in pilgrimage to Saintes-Maries-de-la-Mer. The name "*Caraco*," or "*Carai*," that was given

to them seems to resemble the Spanish curse word "*Carajo*" and its Catalan form, "*Carai*."

52 *Parasites and thieves, you could say.* The author does not share Gounflo-Anguielo's opinion, far too common among the people of the south. Quite the contrary, it seems to him very mistaken regarding the Caraco. The Caraco or Gypsies, remnants of a great nomadic people, are a race attached to its traditions, proud of its customs, observing ancient laws one cannot help but honor if one has any feeling for ethnic mystery and continuity.

53 *Mourraioun.* A sort of muzzle made by gardians, by winding the horse-hair rope or seden, which is part of the equipment, around the horse's nose. The mourraioun, replacing the bit and bridle, is only used when the horse is temporarily ridden bareback.

53 *Coudougnan.* Location in Languedoc.

53 *Séuvo-Riau.* A once wooded region, located on the border of the Little Rhône. Latin: *Sylva Regalis.*

54 *Li Santo.* Saintes-Maries-de-la-Mer. Place made famous by the tradition of the arrival of the Saint Marys in Provence and the annual pilgrimage on the 24th and 25th of May. In the Middle Ages it was called *Sancta Maria de Ratis, Nostra Dona de la Mar,* or *la Villa de la Mar.* Today our people simple call it *li Santo,* the Saints.

55 *Senso bloucage.* Without buckles. The gardian's saddle is held in place by two straps. Surcingles and straps are attached without buckles by little cords laced between two links that form a hoist.

55 *Saquetoun.* Feedbag.

56 *Grau d'Ourgoun.* Gulf of Orgon, in the estuary of the Little Rhône, near Les Saintes-Maries-de-la-Mer.

56 *Narbounés.* The Narbonne wind from the south-southwest, a western breeze.

57 *Anoubloun.* Little *anouble,* or yearling. The anouble is, in the gardian's lingo, a one-year-old bull; at two years, the animal is a *doublen*; at three a *ternen*; at four, a *quatren.*

60 *Sóuvage.* The Sauvage, bull territory located on the left bank of the Little Rhône. It is in the Sauvage that Mistral has Ourrias living:

> *Dóu Sóuvage, negro, malino*
> *E renoumado es la bouvino.* (Mirèio)

Pèire Guilhem's Remorse

63   *These Spanish bullfights.* Aficionados will perhaps find within the incidents in this tale some details designed to surprise, although they in fact correspond to realities observed during that now long-ago time when, in Arles and elsewhere, Spanish-style bull fights were held with crossbred animals from the region. Anti-Southern propagandists from the S.P.D.A. and other theosophists must give up finding here arguments against bullfights in general and especially against the use of picadors. The case of Pavoun, a "bull-horse," is the professional opinion of the gardian Pèire Guilhem, and has nothing to do with the campaigns of Anglo-Saxon origin.

70   *As long as he pics when the time comes and mounts whatever horse he's given.* Let us here underline this apparent exception to the official rules of local bullfights.

71   *Roustan.* Name of an island in the Rhône.

71   *Ferrado.* A ferrado, as everyone knows, is the operation that consists of chasing on horseback in an open field, then overturning, either on foot or while in the saddle using a trident, and then grabbing by the horns the young bull on whom one wants to stamp the owner's brand. Gardians often conduct this chase and this struggle in front of the arena's audience, as a demonstration, or as sportsmen say, an exhibition. The Camargue ferrado is analogous to the games in open fields and the "horn fights" of Thessalian horsemen.

71   *Liço.* A boulevard in Arles.

79   *La Rouqueto.* A neighborhood in Arles.

The Longline

81   *Catigot.* A sort of bouillabaisse made with wine, one of the tastiest and most typical dishes in gardian cuisine.

86   *Coulau.* Seagull, used as a synonym for "oaf."